Praise for *Hom*

"Home is a Made-Up complicated and surprising depths of motherhood and daughterhood while introducing characters who thrill and linger. A tender and exacting debut from an exciting new voice."
—Marie-Helene Bertino, author of *Parakeet*

"Stories that traverse the fraught territories between old conflicts and new starts, old patterns and uncomfortable realizations. Peopled by characters who are as complex and compromised as your own family, this is a lucid and compassionate collection by a writer to watch."
—Cate Kennedy, author of *Like a House on Fire*

"Plank's stories are capacious and evocative, filled with the human dynamics that often are not found in popular discourse. The settings are characters unto themselves and the characters are multi-layered, relatable, and fully realized within the pages of this collection…The characters in this collection are the ones you typically only hear about when someone asks, in hushed tones: 'did you hear about…?' Once you read, you'll be able to say, yes, you have."
—Jennifer Fliss, author of *The Predatory Animal Ball*

"All of the stories feature complex people in pain who feel quite real, and readers who have grappled with dysfunctional family situations in their own lives will certainly find them relatable. Every reader will be able to connect with the feelings of loneliness, betrayal, anxiety, and hostility that recur throughout these works... A poignant and melancholy collection of stories about the constant search for a place to belong."
—*Kirkus Reviews*

Home is a Made-Up Place

Ronit Plank

Text copyright © 2023 by Ronit Plank
All Rights Reserved. Printed in the United States of America

Published by Motina Books, LLC, Van Alstyne, Texas
www.MotinaBooks.com

Library of Congress Cataloguing-in-Publication Data: .
Names: Plank, Ronit
Title: Home is a Made-Up Place
Description: First Edition. | Van Alstyne: Motina Books, 2023

Identifiers:
LCCN: 2022951864

ISBN-13: 979-8-88784-010-9 (paperback)
ISBN-13: 979-8-88784-009-3 (e-book)

Subjects: BISAC:
FICTION / Short Stories (single author)

Cover Design: Josh Durham, Design by Committee
Interior Design: Diane Windsor

For C, T, and A
who I dreamed of

"I am in a spot where I can neither be what I always am nor turn into what I could be."
—Claire Keegan, *Foster*

Contents

House in the Woods

Nicole had been nervous on the flight and the knots in her stomach were still uncoiling as Kevin's truck lumbered along the rural road the last eight miles to the new house. From the airport in Anchorage, he had driven them forty-five miles north on the Glenn Highway, past Palmer, and then continued east for another hour. It was farther away from town, from anything really, than he had explained.

Kevin ran his fingers through the hair at the nape of her neck while he described the place to her and to Mandy who was messing around in the back with the seat belt of her booster. Kevin Jr. was sacked out in his baby car seat and it was about time; he had been inconsolable on both planes over. Nicole leaned into the dozen red roses Kevin had given her at the airport to catch their scent. It had been three months since he had left her and the kids in Vegas for his training on the oil rig but finally, their family was together again.

Where the road narrowed, Kevin slowed and took a right onto a gravel driveway. Several yards ahead was a white-shingled rambler with three cement stairs leading up to a storm door that swung out, half-open over a modest porch. The house sat on seven acres. There was nothing but forest and open space around them, tundra beyond that. And no neighbors either, except the Clarks next door who had sold them the place. They never would have been able to buy otherwise. Bob Clark had helped Kevin get hired at Doyon; he was the one that could make it easier for Kevin to get a contract once he proved himself.

Their plan had always been to leave Vegas. Nicole had never wanted to raise the kids there and now that Kevin's parents were gone, there was no reason to stay. They just needed to save enough money to get out. She took as many telemarketing shifts as she could but Kevin couldn't seem to hang on to any position for long, only odd jobs he picked up here and there. More and more he'd keep himself holed up in the apartment during the days, his mood worsening. It was like he had forgotten who he was, who Nicole knew he could be, and the farther away he got, the angrier and more unpredictable he became. Nothing Nicole did helped him shake it.

Their connection at Doyon Drilling seemed like

the quickest solution. Once Kevin had income and purpose again, she knew things would get better for them. He would have to travel sometimes and there was no question the work would be difficult, but the trade-off was worth it. He left for Alaska just after Kevin Jr. was born.

Before Kevin had the keys out of the ignition, Mandy shrieked and unbuckled the seat belt of her booster. She leaped up the steps, scooted past the partly open storm door, and charged into the house.

Nicole hoisted the baby car seat out of the car and Kevin got their suitcases. "You can leave the door open like that?"

"No, I need to fix that lock again."

The place was about thirteen hundred square feet, double the size of their apartment in Vegas, and smelled like must and dirt and old beer. The bedrooms had wood paneled walls with mirrors on thin sliding closet doors and were mostly bare. Kevin had gotten some furniture second-hand; Nicole brought the baby into the smallest bedroom and laid him in a lightweight portable crib. She hesitated a moment as she looked at Kevin Jr.'s sleeping face, his lips puckering between soft puffy cheeks into a pout, and then she closed the door behind her.

Mandy jumped off her new bed where she had been bouncing and catapulted herself into Kevin's arms. "Can we go next door and see the sled dogs, Daddy?"

He swung her around. "We'll have to wait until the Clarks are home, Buttercup."

Sled dogs. When Kevin first told Nicole the Clarks kept four of them, she thought he was kidding. It was so different from their old life, so storybook-Alaska, she could hardly believe it.

Nicole unzipped her coat on the way over to Kevin who was stamping snow from his boots on the doormat. She shushed Mandy who was still screeching in bionic preschool volume about all the bedrooms.

Kevin's arms had gotten bigger in the three months he had been up on the rig and he looked like a local in his green flannel shirt. His jaw was rough when she ran her hand along it, but underneath, his skin still looked like he'd been dipped in honey.

"Thank you," she said, hugging him, "it's perfect." Her mouth found his. She felt their kiss deepen; his arms tighten around her. For the first time in months, she let her body rest.

"Nic."

"Hmm."

"Nic, they moved the start day up a week for my rig. I'm going in two days."

She pulled away. "Two days? But you said it was two weeks on, two weeks off."

"That was when I was in Beta group, they just switched me to Alpha. You remember, I told you that."

"But we just got here. Can't you tell them you need to go later?"

4

"I can't go later, I have to stay with the team. That's how it works. How I get the choice gigs."

"Two days."

"It'll be all right, it's good news." He kissed her hand. "You'll see."

Nicole moved to the open front door for some air. Older snow, its crisp surface marked with air holes, clung in icy patches on the ground. In the clearing directly in front of the house only three spindly aspen trees had been allowed to grow—the rest were stumps. A house the color of Comet cleaning powder sat two hundred yards away to the left, a chain link fence behind it, a porch in front, woods all around. The trees and houses were flat and cold in the sky's dim light. The last warmth from the sun had flickered out. It was quiet, like the land was holding its breath waiting for night to fall.

After she unpacked and put Mandy to bed, Nicole snuggled next to Kevin who cradled the cooing baby. How was it possible that the man was more handsome now than when they had met? She had been taking care of everything in Vegas by herself for so long, to be with him now, the relief she felt to have them all together again for their new life just like she'd planned, made her giddy. She swaddled the baby, put him in his crib, and rested her hand on his chest until his body sunk into the mattress and he fell asleep.

She felt her way along the hallway back to the master bedroom, her insides fizzing around again.

Kevin's lips were on hers before she made it to the bed, their bodies wrapped around each other in the yellow light of the bedside lamp. The stubble on his jaw scratched her skin as his mouth traveled over all of her. She moved into him, grateful for the weight of his body on hers.

It had always been this way. When they were draped together, the warm scent of him all around her, the part of him she couldn't reach, the part he reserved for himself, seemed to melt away. She could forget how she always wanted more of him, how when he did shift away or fall asleep, she felt it like a kind of loss, a hollow place inside.

They woke after in a late night daze, arms and legs a warm tangle. Nicole switched out the bedside lamp and they got under the covers and found each other again before, finally, they fell into a heavy sleep.

Just after midnight, Nicole woke to a loud keening animal sound from outside, a dog's late night lament. It was sharp in her ears and sounded close. There was barking in excited pitches. One after another the barks came at Nicole, deep, loud, and agitated. Kevin slept through it. The barking turned plaintive, insistent. And there was a rhythm to it; after one dog started the others would join until they quieted. Then one would begin again and the others would join once more.

The baby started crying. Mandy called out. Nicole went to Mandy's room and shushed her in the dark, told her there was nothing to be scared of, it was just

6

the sled dogs. She left her to get Kevin Jr. and rocked him while she sat with Mandy again and rubbed her back.

There was a clanking metal sound and the barking turned into growling. Deep, low, and snarling it rumbled through the dark to their house.

Kevin shuffled into Mandy's room. "What's wrong?"

"The dogs woke them up."

There was another loud growl and then whimpering.

"What's going on out there?" Nicole whispered.

"Probably their son, Jack, feeding them or something."

"In the middle of the night?"

Outside there was shouting and then a high-pitched yelp of pain. The bang of a gate.

Kevin slumped against Nicole while she rocked the baby and tucked Mandy in again, then he got up and went back to sleep. Nicole opened the vinyl roller shades but couldn't see anything in the empty night. She got back into bed with Kevin and fell asleep as the wind picked up, listening to the dogs whining and the rattling of a chain on the gate.

The next day after Nicole nursed the baby they drove into Palmer. Momentary sunlight flickered between quaking aspen and red alder as their truck wound its way to the main road. Nicole couldn't recall ever feeling anything as sharp as the March air in

Alaska. When she took her first breath outside after having been inside the car or the grocery, or at the church where she grabbed a flyer for a weekly moms group, she felt the shock of it in her lungs.

On Sunday morning Nicole strapped the baby to her chest in a carrier and walked with Mandy and Kevin across the dirt space between the two houses. To thank Mr. Clark for helping them, Nicole brought the blueberry muffins she had baked before the kids had woken and Kevin grabbed two cases of beer.

The Clarks' property looked merely disorganized from a distance but as they neared it, Nicole saw it was strewn with a heap of torn window screens, the white square top of a camper, an overturned plastic trash can, an old car engine and a bunch of chewed up sneakers. A "Private Property" sign in orange and black had been stuck near the drive. Beyond it, in front of the house, Nicole counted three "No Trespassing" signs in white letters on black. Dogs barked from behind the chain link fence at the back of the house as they approached.

Kevin knocked. Nicole glanced at the front window but could only see the black garbage bag taped over it. Kevin knocked again. The dogs started in earnest, a crescendo of barks exploded into the air. The gate rattled and Nicole watched the dogs' dark snouts turned sideways, sniffing beneath it.

Nicole shifted her weight and adjusted Kevin Jr. in the baby carrier. Kevin shrugged his shoulders and knocked even louder.

The door opened and Mrs. Clark stared at the baby attached to Nicole's chest. She was taller than Nicole; a faded baggy blue sweatshirt that might have once fit hung open around her neck, revealing a jutting collarbone. A handkerchief held her straight gray hair away from her face. Her light eyes shifted to Nicole without signs of comprehension.

Kevin smiled and introduced the family.

"You brought the whole brood over," Mrs. Clark said.

Nicole laughed a little.

Mrs. Clark peered into the baby carrier, her hand still on the inside doorknob.

"Can we come in and say hi?" Nicole asked.

"I don't see why not." She opened the door and watched as they entered. The sound of cheering and referee whistles blared from a TV somewhere nearby inside the dark house. Mandy held tightly to Nicole's hand, her head pressed into her side.

Cigarette smoke hung in the air, mingling with the smell of bacon grease. Mr. Clark, a thick, heavy-cheeked man with olive colored skin and dark wrinkled circles under his eyes, sat holding a beer in an armchair. His son, Jack, who looked about seventeen, sprawled on a sagging denim couch, opposite, his boots resting on a coffee table thick with old magazines and cans of Pabst and an overflowing ashtray. Nicole squinted and coughed as the smoke hit her eyes.

"Kevin's here," Mrs. Clark announced over the

cheering from the crowd on TV.

"I can see that," Mr. Clark's eyes darted from Mrs. Clark to Kevin. "Was with some of the fellas from your rig over in town last night. Thought you'd be there."

"The family just got here, I've been settling them in. This is Nicole."

"Hi. I made these for you this morning." Nicole smiled at Mr. Clark and offered the plate.

"Muffins," Bob looked at his wife and then Jack. "How about that." His deep-set brown eyes grazed over her. "Sweetie, you can set them down right there, if you can find a place."

Mandy rubbed her eyes and peered through the fog in the living room; the baby kicked his legs against Nicole's abdomen and whined. Nicole lifted him out of the carrier.

"Here," Mr. Clark said gesturing for her to bring the baby to his waiting hands.

"Oh, you don't have to." Nicole said.

"It's fine," he said gesturing again. Nicole brought him over and Mr. Clark held the baby up facing him. "Look at this little guy. You want a beer, Kevin? Ellen, get a beer. Jack, make some room, move your fat ass."

Jack glared at his father from under his dark eyebrows. He had the same thick short hair, but his skin was smooth and doughy. He lowered one foot off the table and then the other and shifted to the far side of the couch. Nicole sat with Mandy next to her watching Kevin Jr. in Mr. Clark's arms. Jack lit another cigarette.

"I'm sorry, Kevin," Mrs. Clark rested her hand on his shoulder and delivered him a beer in her other hand, "we're all out of the Alaskan Amber you brought over last week."

"Kevin, you hear anything yet?" Mr. Clark asked.

"Looks like I might be up for Roughneck, a month on, a month off," Kevin said.

Nicole turned toward him—she hadn't heard about this.

"Mommy," Mandy tugged at Nicole's sleeve while the men continued talking.

A dog howled outside.

"Mommy, can I have a muffin?"

"Jack, excuse me, can you please pass the plate?"

Slumped against the couch armrest, Jack grabbed a muffin with his smoking hand and handed it over to Mandy. A little ash from his cigarette fell onto it.

"Here honey, have this one." Nicole handed a fresh muffin to Mandy, avoiding eye contact with Jack. There was a rattle outside, a bang as a trashcan tipped over and then growling, close, from several dogs.

"Hey shit-for-brains," Mr. Clark yelled at Jack, causing Kevin Jr. to start in his arms, "those dogs get out again?"

"I'll take him," Nicole said, swooping over to get the baby.

Jack looked back at his father frozen, his eyes alert for the first time. He sprinted through the kitchen.

"That's right," Mr. Clark called after him, a thick

ropey vein appearing in the middle of his forehead, "you better run."

"Out! Out of there! Get back!" They heard Jack yelling and he slammed the back door behind him.

Mr. Clark leaned back and pulled out another cigarette.

"You like that house, Nicole?"

She cuddled Kevin Jr. to her, adjusting him in her arms, "It's nice to finally have space." She patted Mandy on the arm while looking for a way to leave without being rude. Mandy nibbled on her muffin and watched the TV. "It's so far away from everything. But, it'll be great. I just need to paint it, add some curtains, fix it up a little, make it feel like home." Nicole bounced Kevin Jr. lightly on her leg.

"We lived there for years. It felt like home didn't it, Ellen?"

Mrs. Clark's glassy eyes stayed on the baby. If she answered, Nicole didn't hear her.

"Hey Kevin," Nicole said and waited for him to look at her before she continued. "I think I need to take Kevin Jr. home for his bottle, he's fussing." Nicole took Mandy's hand and edged her way around the coffee table. "I'm sorry we can't visit longer."

"Bob, I'll stay a while if that's all right."

"You're not coming?" Nicole asked.

"Some of the other guys are coming over." He squeezed her hand. "I'll be home a little later, babe." Kevin led Nicole and the kids to the front door; Mrs. Clark's eyes lingered on their hug goodbye like she was looking for something of hers they'd taken.

Nicole tried to get Kevin to follow her outside where they could talk, but he missed the signal. The door closed.

Nicole's steps seemed too small as she crossed the space between the houses with the baby in her arms and Mandy trailing behind her. When she unlocked the front door it was dimmer inside than she remembered. She clicked on lamp after lamp but the house seemed to swallow up the light.

Kevin got back at four that afternoon, during the baby's nap, smelling like hamburgers, smoke, and beer.

"Hey, babe." He went over and gave Nicole a kiss.

Nicole didn't answer.

"I said hello."

She stared at him from the sofa. "Hi."

Mandy came out of her room singing a song she made up about Alaska. "Daddy!"

"At least somebody's happy I'm home."

Mandy did loops around Kevin while she sang.

"What was that all about?" Nicole asked.

"What?" He kicked off his boots. "Mandy, quit it."

"I thought we were spending your last afternoon together."

"I said knock it off, Mandy. Yeah, I would have liked to."

"Huh."

What do you mean, 'huh'?"

"You would have liked to, you just couldn't tear

13

yourself away from Creepville?"

He gripped Mandy by her shoulders. "I told you to STOP DOING THAT," he said, halting her, his face close to hers.

Mandy looked from Kevin to Nicole. After a moment, he let Mandy go. "I'm going to pack."

Nicole settled Mandy in her room with her dolls and followed Kevin into the bedroom, where he was tossing undershirts and socks into a duffel bag.

She watched him from the door, her arms crossed over her chest. "Why did you stay all afternoon?"

"If Clark puts in a good word for me, I move up."

"And you *have* to get drunk."

"Give me a freaking break, Nicole. Two days and you're already starting." He slammed the dresser drawer closed. "We went over this, right? Every one of the guys on my team wants Roughneck, every one of them. This is how I get it." Kevin zipped up his bag and tossed it onto the rug. "You're just angry because you don't want me to go." He flopped onto the bed. "It's all right, I understand."

He pulled his guitar over from its stand near the window and played the first few chords of the song he'd written for their wedding. "Come over here," he said looking up at her from under his baseball cap and strumming some more. "Nic, don't be that way." He put the guitar aside and patted the blanket next to him. "Come on. Lock the door and come over here."

She had moved away from the door and stood near the foot of the bed, staring at him. She played with a loose thread on the quilt.

"Suit yourself then." He rolled over and rubbed his eyes with the palm of his hand. His voice faded. "But you know you're going to miss me."

"You're unbelievable," she said, shaking her head.

"Get over here." He reached for her hand, and after a moment she let him pull her down toward him.

Just before dinnertime, Kevin's ride came to pick him up. Nicole coaxed Mandy, who had suction-cupped herself to Kevin's back, to sit down and eat her mac 'n cheese and she put the baby down on a blanket.

Kevin clasped his hands around the small of Nicole's back and brought her close.

"I'm not ready to say goodbye," she said, looking up at him.

He brushed the hair away from her eyes and kissed her. "I'll call when I can. Get into town, go to that church group, Nic."

He gave Mandy a hug and picked up his bag. Nicole walked him outside to see him off.

After the truck turned onto the road, Nicole went back inside and closed the storm door behind her. It drifted slowly out again, hanging half open for anything to get in. She balled up a tissue and wedged it between the doorframe and the door and locked it shut.

Nicole didn't see the Clarks the first few days after

Kevin left, but she could always tell when they arrived home because the barking next door became frantic. Mandy still wanted to meet the dogs; she talked about them all the time. About a week into Kevin's rotation Nicole sat on the porch with the baby while Mandy, zipped up in her jacket, her fingers red with cold, built a stone path with rocks she had collected from under the melting snow. Kevin Jr. cooed as he grabbed Nicole's long hair and he giggled every time she feigned surprise at catching him with a pudgy fistful near his mouth.

When they heard Jack's Jeep all of them turned their heads to the road at the same time. Jack screeched up, put it in park, and jumped out. Mandy stood up with a rock in each hand. She threw the rocks down and ran toward Jack. "Can we see the dogs?"

"Mandy, get back here!"

"Can we see them?" Mandy shouted again, gaining on Jack.

Nicole held Kevin Jr. tightly as she caught up to them.

"If you have a minute," Nicole said, breathing hard, "She's never seen a team of sled dogs."

Jack, a hand on his porch railing, looked from mother to daughter with dead eyes. "They're just dogs. We don't run them." When Nicole and Mandy made no move to leave he shook his head and turned towards the fence with them following. "There are just two now. The others got hurt."

16

As she approached the fence, the smell of dog excrement rolled over Nicole in waves. Green plastic board ran four feet high around the circumference of the enclosure. A chain with a dangling padlock secured it shut. Piles of dog droppings were strewn around the dirt yard. Two skinny dogs barreled over to Jack, barking loudly. The first was a tall gray husky; the second, a black and white, limping, her right hind paw caked with dried blood.

"Sit!" Jack commanded. He opened the padlock and swung the gate open halfway. Mandy and Nicole stayed behind him. The dogs' muzzles sniffed the air, searching, their cloudy eyes focused, as they shifted from front paw to front paw while also trying to edge closer to Jack and the open gate. Their fur was matted and missing in some places. Their skin hugged their ribs, rippling over each boney arch in a shiver. Yellow discharge ran from the injured dog's right eye. Both dogs whined and sniffed, saliva falling in steady drops from their muzzles and gums. They did not look at all like the majestic dogs she had seen in photographs.

"What happened to that one's paw?" Mandy asked.

"She was trying to get more than her share. This guy put her in her place."

"They fight over food?" Nicole asked.

"Only when they're fed." He was looking down at the dogs as they furiously searched the ground, near Nicole and Mandy's shoes, then the baby's feet, for something to lick, to eat. Just as Jack moved to close the gate, the big grey dog slid past his legs, halfway out of the enclosure. Jack barred the dog's way with his boot. Once the dog started to back up, Jack kicked at his muzzle. The dog tried once more and Jack kicked at him again. The dog ducked low and whimpered. "Back!" Jack shouted. He slammed the gate.

"Will she be able to pull the sled?" Mandy asked.

Jack looked at her like she had just appeared. "What?"

"The hurt one."

"Yeah," he said, and started toward the house. "Sure."

"Don't you need to put the lock on the gate?" Nicole asked and then felt immediately guilty. The poor dogs would be lucky to escape.

Jack stopped. Without looking at Nicole he came back, clicked the lock into place, and stalked back to the house.

Her fingers looped through chain link, Nicole watched the dogs until Mandy reached for her hand and pulled her away to go home. But even as she drew the shades that night and got the kids ready for bed, Nicole thought of the dogs. The look in their eyes stayed with her.

That week she and the kids drove the hour for the church playgroup in Palmer. The women there were all originally from Alaska. They looked like they could chop a hundred trees, fire a shotgun, and turn around and make their own granola. And they all knew each other. Nicole wiped her lipstick off and tied her blonde hair back beneath a baseball cap, but she still felt out of place.

The second time she went she did get to talk to this woman Jill, who seemed to know everybody, and suggested they exchange phone numbers. But when the playtime was over and Nicole and Mandy were cleaning up big plastic dinosaurs with missing teeth and broken tails, Jill waved and left with the group. It was fine, Nicole told herself, it would be fine. These things took time.

That spring she re-grouted the tub and sink and painted the bathroom. She lay down new linoleum in the kitchen and re-stained the table. When she went to town she made sure to take lots of time running her errands so she could meet more people before she and the kids made the long drive back home. But conversations were rushed and almost always interrupted. She called friends back in Vegas, but they rarely answered their phones.

Nicole counted down the hours whenever Kevin was due home. She'd get the house ready and bake and she always put on something nice to wear. When he was back, she stayed in bed with him as long as she could before the kids needed her. His return gave shape to her life. She made pancake breakfasts for him and the kids and huge dinners. Sometimes she got Kevin to go on a drive or hike but mostly he preferred to take it easy on his time off. Or he would visit the Clarks. He went over there more and more now that it was down to just him and one other guy up for Roughneck. But she tried to be grateful; she had never seen him so motivated. His five months on the rig represented the longest he'd ever held onto a job.

The nights were hardest when Kevin was away. At the end of the day, after she'd locked up the windows and doors and put the kids to bed, she'd send an email or two if the Internet wasn't down, or sit in front of the TV for reruns, but it didn't stop the unsettled, empty place inside her from growing. She was unnerved by the amount of night around her; the sharp cries of the dogs trapped in their pen, waiting for someone to come.

During Kevin's third trip away she took the note she had written and hoisted the jumbo bag of dog food she'd bought on sale out of her trunk and lugged it over to the Clark's back porch. It didn't look like they were home but, just in case, she tore open the waxy paper and quickly scooped out a third of the bag. She tossed the kibble through the cracks in the fence and covered her ears until the dogs stopped their barking long enough to eat. She left the remainder of the bag and the note on the Clark's back porch. Two days later the remaining bag of food was back on her front steps, unused.

In June, Kevin got the news: He was moving up to Roughneck, a month on, a month off, starting immediately. He wouldn't be home until the afternoon of Mandy's fifth birthday.

The night before he left, Nicole prepared a bon voyage dinner in honor of his promotion. With a lump in her throat she moved around her small kitchen roasting chicken and baking bread. Late that night, after they'd finished their bottle of champagne, Kevin kissed her and said he'd see her a little later; he had a case of beer for Bob Clark, to thank him for the help.

Lying in the middle of the bed, not expecting sleep, she left the blackout shades up in her bedroom and watched leaf shadows shimmy across her walls in the withering light. It felt like little pieces of her were coming apart—her chest shook with the effort of holding them all together.

When Kevin woke up the next day and came into the kitchen he had only a few hours before he had to leave.

"Morning guys," he said.

Nicole scrubbed at the bacon gristle stuck to the pan.

"Thanks for letting me sleep."

Nicole put the pan on the shelf and slammed the cabinet door shut.

"Anything you need me to do before I go?"

She walked out of the room.

"Hey."

She moved into the bedroom and snapped the sheets off the mattress.

He came in. "I'm talking to you."

"Terrific."

"What's your problem?"

21

"What's my problem?" She threw the pile of sheets to the floor. "You're never here is my problem!"

"Hey, back up. This job was your idea, remember?"

"Spending all your time at the Clarks was not my idea!"

"I'm busting my ass for this family. For you!"

"You are leaving us for a month. A month!"

Mandy came into their bedroom. "Mommy?"

"Out," Kevin said.

"But I wanted to ask Mommy,"

"I'm going to count to three."

"But, Daddy," He moved toward her and her eyes filled with tears. She stammered, "I need to ask—"

"That's it." He picked her up and put her in her room and slammed the door. "Stay there until I tell you to get out."

Nicole shook her head. She walked out of the room to get the baby who had started crying out of his crib.

"It's only a month, Nicole." Kevin yelled after her.

When his ride pulled up two hours later, Kevin brought his bag to the door. After he put his jacket on, he brushed Nicole's cheek with the back of his hand. "We'll talk about it when I come home, all right?" He hugged the three of them goodbye and left. Nicole sat on the sofa staring at the road until Mandy asked her about dinner.

Nicole had unpacked all the boxes and organized and painted the house, and now there was almost nothing to do. She made weekly trips to Palmer to meet Jill and the other ladies she was becoming friendly with from the church, but she didn't talk with them about how hard it was living so far from anyone. How slowly the last three and a half weeks on her own had gone. They weren't those kinds of friends, or at least, no one seemed to talk like that.

With summer, the light in the sky hung on until it dwindled into the faint glow of early morning and then started all over again. At night, after Kevin had called for their brief conversation, she sat in front of the TV and drank beer until she got buzzed enough or it got dark enough to try to sleep. There seemed to only be bits left of what she and Kevin had once had. She didn't know what she was trying to build anymore.

The night before Mandy's birthday, the day Kevin was finally due home, Nicole sat on the porch. She looked up and out of the woods to the farthest place her eyes could reach. Where the tops of the tallest evergreens scaled the sky, their dark jagged outlines silhouetted against a gray-white shot through with the streaky gold of perpetual sunset. They looked so high and so far away, the space above them so endless, Nicole's heart skipped. She was struck with a feeling of floating above, of getting away. It was an ache inside her.

The next morning Nicole drove the hour to Palmer with the kids. She got some more flowers to plant in the front yard and she splurged on good wine and the best cuts of beef available. Jill and her family were coming over for Mandy's birthday celebration; they still hadn't met Kevin. Nicole hummed to herself all day while she baked the cake and cleaned the house. Then she painted Mandy's nails and her own in celebration.

The night was warm and they sat outside while the kids ran around. Jill and her husband were from Anchorage; they wanted to hear all about Vegas. They got Nicole to talk about her old telemarketing days— the bizarre stories she'd heard from the showgirls who worked alongside her when their stints were up. How small her and Kevin's apartment was, how they had to keep the air conditioning blasting and their mouths nearly always tasted like Freon, how Kevin insisted on Foreman-grilling all their dinners on their teeny stamp-sized balcony.

Kevin Jr. fell asleep in Nicole's arms and she kissed him and put him in his crib while the big kids stayed up late playing hide and seek behind the trees. Later, when it started to drizzle, they all went inside, leaving the doors and windows open for air.

They held dinner as long as they could that night waiting for Kevin to get back from his review. After he called to say he would definitely be there, but was running late, Nicole served their dinner, putting aside large helpings of everything for Kevin. And then, checking the road one last time, she lit Mandy's birthday candles and served the cake.

By eleven everybody was full and drowsy. They had finished the wine and gone back for seconds. Jill's little girl and Mandy had fallen asleep on the sofa leaning against each other. Nicole and Jill gently dislodged their daughters, and, wobbling under the weight of the sleeping girls, said good night. Nicole carried Mandy to her room and her friends let themselves out.

Nicole propped open Kevin Jr.'s door to get some air circulating now that it was quiet. His head was turned toward her, his sweet, feathery breath blowing softly in and out. She switched off his lamp and went down the hall to turn off the other lights in the house. She'd forgotten how much she loved having people over—to have friends with her for a whole evening felt like being alive. Jill and her husband said they couldn't believe Kevin had bought a house so far away from Palmer. Nicole was going to talk to him about that tonight, if he ever got home. They would have to at least move to Sutton where Jill lived.

When Nicole returned to the living room to lock up the door the light of her cell phone caught her eye. She had missed a call from Kevin. When she called back he didn't answer. His voicemail message was hard to follow; garbled music and shouts sounded in the background but she heard something about a bar, still being in Anchorage, Bob Clark and some of the guys on the board, "tell Mandy I love her…celebrate tomorrow."

It felt like she'd been punched. She slammed her

phone onto the table. She picked it up again and listened to the message once more and threw it against the wall. She was so stupid. So stupid to have thought he would make it back to be with them. With her.

She tried to catch her breath but she couldn't calm through her tears. She let her body drop to the couch and the living room blurred up around her. She didn't know what they had anymore; if he'd ever felt about her the way she felt about him. Her breath finally slowed enough for her to sleep.

A noise woke her. A cry.

She sat up. Her scalp tingled.

Something wasn't right.

"Kevin?" she called out, but there was no answer. "Kevin?"

The front door was swung wide open. Mud was tracked in on the floor. From near the bedrooms she heard a breathy lapping sound. A low grunting. Her stomach clenched.

She hadn't locked up the house.

She crept down the hall and flipped on Mandy's light. Mandy had thrown her blankets off and was asleep, soundly. Nicole covered her back up.

From the hallway Nicole heard a scratching sound, like fingernails on wood. It grew louder as she got closer to the baby's room. In the dark she fumbled for the switch to Kevin Jr.'s brass lamp. When she clicked on the light there was a growl.

The crib had been pushed sideways against the wall. Kevin Jr.'s arm stuck out from the bars—the sleeve of his yellow onesie was torn. Next to him the big gray dog from the Clarks pushed his snout between the bars, pulling at the mattress with his teeth. The black and white dog crouched at the foot of the crib watching him. Keeping one eye on Nicole, the gray dog sniffed at Kevin Jr. as he slept, licking at his exposed skin.

Nicole reached for the lamp on the table behind her. Ripping the cord out of the wall, she flipped it upside down. At her movement the gray dog bared his teeth. The black and white dog inched closer to Kevin Jr. and the gray dog snarled at her. His mouth opened around Kevin Jr.'s arm. Just as it was about to close Nicole lifted the lamp high and slammed it into the grey dog's accordion ribs. He yelped but did not move from the baby. Nicole raised the lamp above her head and she struck at his neck, lashed again at his ribs. Whimpering now, he cowered to the wood floor.

Nicole swung to face the black and white dog but she had shrunk to the corner.

Nicole's hands were trembling; going numb. She tried to make her fingers move but they felt nerveless, jointless, as if filled only with air. The lamp dropped to the floor.

Shrieking, she kicked at the dogs with her feet. Her bare toes registered their sunken hindquarters, the bristle of their fur, the feel of their bony bodies' loose, sliding skin.

She drove the crouching dogs to the front door. The gray dog made it outside but his breathing was staggered. He managed the porch steps, but after a few limping paces he slowed, tracking Nicole with pale, desperate eyes. The black and white dog paused next to him.

Tails and haunches tucked low, the dogs lifted their snouts and breathed in the dim morning. The gray dog coughed a hacking sound. His eyes returned to Nicole. She stared back. After a moment he turned and began a ragged trot toward the Clarks'. The black and white dog followed, limping.

Nicole stepped off the porch. She shouted for them to stop. They quickened their pace and she found herself going after them, moving faster, yelling. They swerved to avoid her, but she cut them off. Each time, she blocked their path to the Clarks.

She had them going the other way now. Tears streaming down her face, she chased them out to where the stand of trees bordering the property began. She ran them into the thicket, screaming at them to go.

Later, when Nicole let herself think about what had happened to all of them, how she'd left Kevin and how Mandy watched her with worried eyes; when she felt like she couldn't breathe, she thought about the dogs.

They had wanted, needed so badly.

They must have crept out of their pen that night sniffing the soil, the detritus, for something to eat, garbage, a bone, an old carrot. Smells must have poured into their dry black snouts, saturating their starved brains. Their paws touching lightly down and, pushing back against the packed mud, they went searching for sustenance. And then, on the wind: the scent of another house. The smell of other lives.

Nicole would remember how she had watched them moving farther and farther away that last morning until finally, free and wild with hunger, their bodies disappeared into the woods.

Gibbous

You pull up in front of Wade's school, slam your car door, and take the steps two at a time. Your to-go coffee slips from your fingers in front of the main entrance and spills all over the pavement. Brown blotches splatter your best dress; wet floral fabric clings to your shins. You bend down toward the steaming cement to pick up the crushed Styrofoam and curse yourself, imagining the impression you're going to make tromping into the building messy and breathless, to remind the principal you have Wade's condition under control.

The school called you to come get Wade during your shift at Oasis Spa, in the middle of giving a massage. Apparently, when another boy had touched Wade's arm during basketball Wade screamed and pushed him down. You seriously doubt the boy was injured; Wade is the small-lest kid in school by a head. All the steroids in his asthma inhalers and ADHD medicines have slowed his growth. The last specialist that saw him took some high-tech photo of his hand and determined that his bones were two years younger than his actual age: he is the size of a six-year-old. But, he wouldn't stop screaming until they brought him to the nurse. He has a fever now and Principal White said the wounds on Wade's body are swollen and infected looking, almost like boils.

Tucson's spring has been especially hard on his allergies this year. Bumpy patches of eczema, some light pink and raw, some scabbed over and cranberry-colored, march over his body, tickling and teasing him, begging to be touched. He digs in and scratches deeply, rhythmically. Like a strange meditation, the scratching soothes him. But it only makes his condition worse. He has to soak in a bath and put his steroid ointments on right away, or his skin splits and stings.

You dump your battered and dripping cup into a trashcan, wipe the coffee from your legs with an old tissue from your bag, and walk into the building. This is the fourth time the school has called you in this year; it seems like everything with them is an emergency. But you can't keep missing work—there's only so much your manager will understand.

Just outside the principal's door, Wade sits slumped in a worn wooden chair near a corner, looking out the window, his jaw snapping the way it does when he's upset, his dust brown bangs in his eyes.

"Hi baby." You brush his hair away from his forehead. He is warm. "Mom," he says and grabs onto your hand to hold it. "I'll be right back," you tell him and you kiss his papery cheek.

You straighten your skirt and pop your head into Principal White's office. He sits behind his uncluttered desk, a thick file open in front of him, his brow pinched in concentration. Wade's teacher, Mrs. Sutton, is also there in one of two green-cushioned chairs, her gray hair twisted up neatly as usual, her readers on the very tip of her nose. When you knock on the putty-colored doorway to announce your arrival she turns, smiles briefly at you, and then faces forward again.

"Sorry, I got here as soon as I could."

"That's fine, Johanna," Principal White answers.

Before you can sit, he and Mrs. Sutton launch into the trouble with Wade.

"It was my fault," you interrupt. "I shouldn't have skipped his bath last night. I promise he won't show up to school again with any infections. I'll have his dermatologist put him on something right away."

As if synchronized, their looks of concern become tinged with frustration. They didn't call you in because of his skin. Principal White pulls the file close to him, flips through the papers and reads through the various dates in the last two months Wade has been out of control. Beads of sweat pop out over your top lip.

Mrs. Sutton shifts in her seat so she is facing you. She tilts her head to the side in the way people do to emphasize their concern. "We feel something more may need to be evaluated."

"It would be a good idea for you to see a specialist." Principal White says and asks Mrs. Sutton for the referral. "Dr. Schuyer works with a lot of families like yours."

"What does that mean?"

"Parents who need more support."

Heat prickles over your cheeks. "You know, I appreciate that but Wade and I have been through these hiccups before. We can handle it."

Principal White and Mrs. Sutton share a look and he clears his throat. "We anticipate you're going to need more guidance during this time. Dr. Schuyer can help you navigate all the different diagnoses on the spectrum."

"The spectrum?"

"Yes. The autism—"

"Wait." You are sure your face is red now. "Wait. That is not what's going on here. I told you, I just need to get serious with his meds again."

Mrs. Sutton shifts her eyes from you to Principal White who looks down at his folded hands before saying finally, "Johanna, Wade needs to be seen. Dr. Schuyer is the doctor the school district recommends."

As soon as you've exited the office you shove the

referral into your purse. Wade does not need another evaluation. The school just needs to learn how to handle him already.

"Wade, honey?" You give his shoulder a little squeeze.

"Yeah, Mommy?"

"It's time to go."

Wade has one foot in the tub and one foot out, and bathwater is everywhere. You edge him back into the tub but he rises out of the water again, shivering, his jaw snapping more urgently than usual.

You hold onto his mottled arms. "Wade," you speak as calmly as you can, your face close to his ear, "you have to get in." You press him down toward the bath and quickly, before he gets up again, you splash water on his neck with a plastic bowl. He screams in an otherworldly decibel and you wonder again how so much sound can come from such a tiny, damaged chest. He snatches the bowl out of your hands and throws it at you. You jam your lips together to hold back the words about to explode out of your mouth and clamp his arms down at his sides. He kicks a slippery leg out of the tub, climbs out, and runs down the hallway toward his bedroom, his skinny, bendy-straw limbs flailing.

"Damn it, Wade!" you yell. "Get back here!" Exhausted, you yank the towel off the hook. "You're going to slip," you say, but know he can't hear you anymore. With heavy steps you start your ten count and trudge down the narrow hall.

Photos of you and Wade, your late mother and Wade, and Wade and his dog before you'd had to give the dog away because of Wade's allergies, are on the left wall. Framed drawings Wade made are on your right. For the longest time he drew his people's mouths as lines straight across—he couldn't seem to make the curve of a smile. You remember how that was something you used to worry about, back before his ADHD was diagnosed, before your mother died, before you were so much on your own. You shake your head. Now it would be a gift to worry about something as small as that.

You follow sloppy, wet footprints into his small room where they end at his bed. He is naked and huddled underneath. A gray dust bunny clings greedily to his pointy elbow. "Come out, baby."

He stares at you.

"Come out before you dry up so we can get your medicine on you."

His jaw snaps twice, fast.

You sit on your heels, your head jammed under the bed, and try several more times. Leaning on your haunches in the darkening room, your forearms resting on your thighs, your thighs flattened against your calves, your body settles a little. It is a comfort to stop moving. A kind of peace. When Wade looks this bad you need to slick him with ointments, get him into his pajamas, and put socks onto his hands and feet so he won't scratch his skin open in his sleep. You have to duct tape the socks on so he won't peel them off; he's so hot all the time he can barely stay in his clothes.

And he calls for you at least once a night—the itching is always worse then. You rest next to him half asleep until his eyes close and his breathing settles. You pick apart your gummy thoughts, trying to make your head work so you can figure out what else you can do to make his life better.

Like you always tell him, it's going to get easier, you just have to get through some more hard stuff for a while.

You refocus your eyes on the naked heap in front of you. Wade's skin is drying fast; you have to get his medicine on him.

At work the following week syrupy harp chords drip into the darkened spa room. You try not to listen. Music pumps in through the speakers from nine in the morning to nine at night, some of it relaxing, most of it cloying. It reminds you of big breezy windows and white curtains rippling from intermittent ocean breezes, a place of comfort you've never been, would be lucky to someday go.

You smooth more massage oil on your client's fleshy back and press firmly. You breathe in and out with each motion, moving your hands around the broad surface. The skin is supple and healthy, resilient, almost like rubber. How different everybody is. You make impossible bargains in your head, dream bargains. You are always searching for the right formula, as if coming up with one would make it true. If Wade had skin like this lady's, even a fifth like this lady's, his body would be unbroken, impermeable to air, dust, food, animals, stress. He could be a superhero.

That night you speak to Mrs. Sutton on the phone while you make dinner. She called to discuss the end of school field trip and sleepover to Sabino Canyon, the trip the entire first grade goes on that Wade's been talking about all year. It's less than a month away and you are grateful she wants to help make it possible for him to come. She knows what it means to him, what it means to you, and you thank her. Wade tugs on your shirt. He keeps interrupting to ask if there will be horses on the trip to the Canyon. He loves horses. Finally you give him a juice box and tell him to go entertain himself while you arrange the sleepover details. With your work schedule field trips are nearly impossible, but this is special. And with all his allergies to animals and dust and pollen, you have to be there.

When the pasta is ready, you put it on the table and finish your conversation with Mrs. Sutton. You call Wade in but he doesn't answer.

You look out of the kitchen window. He isn't in the front yard. You call him again. The house is quieter than it was before. You feel a twinge inside. Whenever it's too quiet, something is up.

You wipe your hands on the kitchen towel and walk down the hall. Wade isn't in his bedroom or his closet. You go into your room but don't find him there either, so you walk back into the hall and call him again. You hear the sound of running water from behind the bathroom door. You knock. He doesn't answer. You knock again and open the door. Wade is standing in the tub, eyebrows furrowed, wearing only his Incredible Hulk underwear, scouring his body with your loofah scrub brush.

Everywhere he has been scrubbing, everywhere his crusty patches have been, is now raw and shining. You try to keep your voice level and ask him what he is doing. He looks up, holds out the brush. With twinkling eyes he tells you he is getting rid of his bad skin. "We have to give it a chance to grow back better, Mommy."

You can't swallow past the hard rock in your throat. You don't know where to begin; he has shallow holes, new wounds all over him. The rawness of him stabs at you like cold metal. How will it ever heal?

You can't put his clothes on and you can't put him in the bath to clean him. You squeeze out the rest of the antibiotic ointment you have lying around from his last staph infection and smear it on wet bandages. But your hands feel thick and clumsy, your fingers like the rolls of coins the machine at the grocery store spits out.

Wade gets into his booster seat for you but screams when you inch the seatbelt around him to drive to the drugstore to pick up more prescription antibiotic ointment. You drive, not seeing anything you're looking at. If only you could just take off parts of yourself you didn't want, simply rip them off and start fresh.

You miss the next three days at the spa to take care of him. You hope your clients will understand. You call Dr. Schuyer's office and book his first available appointment two weeks from now.

It is more than a week before Wade's skin begins to harden up again. Now his body is flecked with thick dark scabs. You remind him over and over and over to stop scratching so he can get better and go on the Sabino Canyon trip with the rest of his class. "You can do this," you tell him.

On the morning of your appointment with Dr. Schuyer you pick up some donuts and chocolate milk for Wade. He tells about a hundred knock-knock jokes while he eats and you laugh at almost all of them, which gets him going too, so he tells another and then another. In your rearview mirror you see his big grin, the dimple on his left cheek back in its place. That is your real son, the one you can have most of the time if you could just get everything under control.

Dr. Schuyer's office is in a behemoth of a government building. No air looks like it can get past the jutting cement slabs that surround the recessed, already narrow windows; the elevator smells stale and faintly of industrial cleaning solution.

The doctor asks for a private interview with you. He has already spoken with Wade who is now sprawled out on the waiting room floor. The fluorescent overhead lights cast him in an unhealthy shade of beige as he sifts through a basket of plastic toys, pressing buttons and clicking on/off switches, searching for one with good batteries. These places never replace their batteries. That breaks your heart a little more. Why can't everything just work the way it's supposed to?

You ask the receptionist to keep an eye on Wade and then you follow Dr. Schuyer to his office. You're used to these professional assessments—you've been going to them since Wade's ADHD diagnosis two years ago.

Dr. Schuyer asks about your daily routines for Wade's care, his diet, sleep patterns, hobbies. You report everything back effortlessly, checking out his office when he looks down to take notes. It's filled with furniture from the eighties; everything in it is a dim orange-brown. A bulky dinosaur of a computer appears as if it is about to practice-ally lunge off his desk.

There is a family photo of the doctor and his wife sitting, each with an infant in their arms, and a blond boy, about eleven, standing between them. All of them smile so certainly, like there's nothing to worry about.

"And," the doctor puts his pen on his clipboard and studies you from under his thick eyebrows, "how do you take care of yourself?"

You stare at him. No one has ever asked you before.

You run a hand through your short brown hair. "Um, I like to read. I have a little backyard with sort of a garden." Your voice surprises you, it sounds thin. You push it to a lower register. "I try to do stuff out there."

Dr. Schuyer is quiet. He is still looking at you. "What happened to your cheek?"

Your hand flies up to the raised red welts Wade's fingernails carved into your skin. They are almost a week old but you can still feel the four tracks sliding down your face on their way to your jaw. They fade into shallow pale pink lines where Wade finally lost his grip and let go. He never purposely tried to hurt you before. "I was giving Wade a bath. It was bad timing." You clear your throat, but can only speak in a whisper. "I wasn't paying attention—" You look down at your lap.

"Nobody expects you to be able to handle this by yourself, Johanna."

Tears begin to drop onto your folded hands.

Dr. Schuyer passes you tissues.

"I just want him to stop fighting me. I want him to let me take care of him." You wipe at your face, try to steady your breath. "You work with this kind of kid, you know they're not always like this. He just needs his medicine adjusted, maybe some play therapy until he feels all right."

"I'm not sure that is the case. Wade shows definite sensory integration and processing dis-orders. Caring for him may actually get more complicated."

You feel like someone is coming for you with a black hood in their hands. You don't know how this happened. How did this happen? The hood is slipping over your head, blotting out the light.

"Johanna?"

You hear Dr. Schuyer tell you he's adjusting Wade's current meds and adding a new one. You understand he is handing you a copy of his preliminary assessment. Call to schedule a diagnostic, he tells you. You take it and nod, and then nod again, like if he would just stop talking, you could go make the call already. But you don't. You can't. Everything has gone dark.

On the morning of the Sabino Canyon trip you make sure Wade has his Claritin as soon as you get to school. Mrs. Sutton has offered to ride with you and Wade and you appreciate it. You notice the other moms driving today, mostly stay-at-homes you don't really know, follow you with their eyes as you walk Mrs. Sutton to your car.

Wade is excited; he interrupts your conversation with his teacher and bounces around in his booster— as much as he can manage with his seat belt on—the whole trip. You drive out of town thirty miles. Away from strip malls with "for lease" signs smashed to their front windows and clusters of homes on evenly spaced plots of dehydrated land. Past tall Saguaro cacti and up the mountain where trees are able to grow again.

The kids wind up the canyon together in pairs, knapsacks and sleeping bags on their backs. Every few pairs, moms clump together talking, watching out for their assigned kids. You don't know many of them but you smile. Good to see you again, you say.

Ten minutes in, Wade runs ahead and points to the trail. "Horse poop! I found horse poop!" and the kids all say, "Eeew." The loamy soil is dry, dust springs up around the group as you walk. Loose pebbles and rocks clunk against each other wherever you step. Dried out lichen, flat and blanched, covers the trunks of the trees that line the path.

When the class gets to the rest area, you and the other mothers lay everything out under the shadiest cottonwood trees you can find while the kids throw Frisbees. Wade runs happily to retrieve the shiny green disk when it lands far away. He is having a great time. He keeps calling out, "I got it, I got it!" putting his hand out so the other kids won't have to race after it into the shrubs. Mrs. Sutton motions to you if it is okay for Wade to be exerting himself and you nod.

While the kids are eating, a couple comes to the rest area and ties up their horses. The kids gather close to them. Wade gets up and you follow him. The man tells the kids all about the horses, how the white one is feisty and the gray one is a slowpoke. He sees Wade's mouth wide open, his eyes glittering as he stares at them. The man asks Wade if he can keep an eye on their rides while he and his wife get some water. You smile your thanks for his kindness. You rest your hand on Wade's shoulder so he won't forget and touch them.

Wade doesn't take his eyes off of the animals, he doesn't move. When the pair remounts and rides down to follow a trail along a dry streambed, Wade follows them. He watches until they are out of sight and then he stays in the dusty streambed with the other kids to search for treasures while you and the other parent chaperones talk and pack up lunch.

Out of the spa in the sun, you are like a regular mom watching your son be a regular kid. A hot breeze rattles the dry hanging leaves above you. With the wind ruffling your hair and the flutter you have inside, you no longer feel fragile, no longer like prey standing unprotected in open desert for any predator to come swoop you away. For once you are unafraid.

Wade calls to you. He runs up the hill breathing heavily, his pants bursting with all the things he's collected from the streambed. Sticks and leaves dangle out of his pockets. Several small rocks drop out near his feet when he rubs his face. "Gentle, Wade," you remind him and you two walk with the class back down the trail to set up camp. Wade lags behind, coughing. He is covering his eyes as he walks.

"What is it, honey?"

You make your way to him, but not soon enough. He stumbles on a rock. When he moves his hands out to catch himself, you see his eyes are swollen and red. He reaches for them again as soon as he regains his balance but you pull his hands down to stop him. He

44

snatches his hands away from you and digs into his eyes with his fingers. His eyelids have puffed out almost as far as his forehead; they are almost on the same plane. His clavicle hollows and his collarbones jut out with each breath he tries to take.

You break open a tab of antihistamine from your backpack and give it to him along with his inhaler. You tell Mrs. Sutton you need to get off the mountain and you pick Wade up. Mrs. Sutton calls to the other moms and follows you; she offers to drive.

Wade cries between breaths. Twigs and pebbles drop from his pockets. You run with him in your arms for the last quarter mile and make it to the car panting and coated in sweat.

Wade coughs and scratches frantically at his arms and his throat. He pulls away from you as you buckle him into his booster. "No, Mommy, no! I can't see!"

"Wade, listen to me. Try to take a breath."

Hives have sprung up on his neck. He moans and bats at the window on his side, slapping his hand against it harder and harder.

"Make it go away!"

You sit next to him in the back and hold his arms down as firmly as you can. You shush him loudly, an aggressive shush right in his ears so he can hear you. Mrs. Sutton starts the car, checking on you in the rearview mirror as the car winds down the mountain.

"I don't know why the inhaler isn't working. Wade, listen to me, did something sting you?"

"No!" Wade heaves himself forward in his booster, swings his head around to shake away the swelling, and screams at a volume you are sure Mrs. Sutton never heard before, surely never in such a small space.

"Wade, did you touch the horses? Mrs. Sutton, did you see him pet the horses?"

Wade sobs, "I didn't, Mom."

"Okay, Honey."

"Just the hair I found."

"What hair?" You are off the mountain now; abruptly the desert surrounds you, cacti sprung up on either side of the highway. "What hair, Wade?"

Wade gasps for a breath, "From the dirt."

You let Wade's arms go. While he swats at you, you rummage through his pockets. You pull out a matted clump of white horse hair the size of a golf ball. Your stomach clenches. You call to Mrs. Sutton over the seat, "I need to get him to the ER."

Hands trembling, you fumble with the cap to the EpiPen. You lay your torso on Wade's lap to hold him still. You clutch the leg closest to the car door and squeeze it to find the fleshiest part. You plunge the needle into his bony thigh and Wade screams a worn-out scream.

Wade is drowsy but you can see a tiny piece of his brown iris now that his eyes are returning to a smaller size. You spent six hours at the hospital before you were released. When you make it home you get Wade settled on the couch and turn on cartoons. You kiss his head and go into the kitchen to heat a can of tomato soup for dinner. When it's ready you walk him into the kitchen, put a bowl in front of him, and sit next to him at the table.

Wade reaches for his spoon. "When are we leaving for the sleepover?"

You pick dried food off the shiny yellow tablecloth.

"Mom?"

"I don't know."

"We're still going, right?"

You rest your elbow on the table and prop your face in your hand. "Eat your dinner, Wade."

He looks up at you. "But we're still going."

"I don't think so."

"No. We are!"

"I said I don't think so."

"NO!" He throws his spoon against the wall; it lands on the floor with a tinny clang.

You place the spoon firmly on the table. "Sit down."

He throws it again.

"Pick it up, Wade."

"Not until you say I can go."

"I am not going to."

He knocks over his water glass. "You better!"

"Damn it, Wade!" You get up to avoid the water running off the plastic tablecloth. You wipe most of it up with a damp kitchen towel. "Sit down and eat your soup right now." When he doesn't move, you grab him by the shoulders and sit him in his chair.

"Ouch! You hurt me!"

"I'm sorry."

"Bad mom!"

"I am not a bad mom."

He stands up again and knocks his chair over. "You are a bad mom!

"No I am not. All I do is take care of you!"

"I don't want you to!"

"Too bad, Wade! You don't get to choose." You turn his chair right side up and slam it into place, tears in your eyes. "Do you understand? We're stuck!" You walk out of the kitchen and just before you slam your bedroom door you yell, "Get ready for bed!"

It's nine o'clock when you come out of your room to check on him, but he is already asleep.

He's so little, lying there. His toothbrush is on his night table. Ointment shines on his skin in the places he was able to reach by himself. He has never done that before.

You go back out to the living room. The house is so quiet.

You sit on the couch and eat the cold soup, pushing aside the orangey red film that has formed on top. Through your window a gibbous moon gleams. An ugly, clumsy name for an ugly, awkward phase of the moon. It has risen, all misshapen, with part of its left side gone. Does that mean it's waxing or waning? You can't remember.

You wake up at three o'clock. Wade is usually up

by now for medicine or cuddling. You miss him. You walk to his room and hear jagged breathing coming from inside.

When you open the door, his legs are dangling off the bed, his sheets are twisted around him from tossing all night. He lies as still as he can. His chest rises up and down.

You move closer. "Baby, what is it?"

You feel his head and chest. "You're hot. Why didn't you come get me?"

He rubs and rubs the inside of his cracked wrist against the sheet. His jaw snaps.

"Wade?"

He turns his head away. "I wish I was never born."

"Wade—" You try to force your voice away from stretched out and breaking so that everything won't tumble out of control, away from the steady place you take care of him. You gather him in your arms.

He rests his head against your shoulder. You cushion his quaking body until he stills. His breathing begins to slow.

"You can't make it better," he says, almost in a whisper.

You sweep your fingertips across his forehead wiping the tears that have streamed down his cheeks and into his hair. Your lips tremble. "That's not true Wade. It's not true."

Not at Home

Dad finally made his way from the front door into the hall and stopped to hold onto our wall for support. His gout-filled cinderblock feet hardly lifted as he tried to cross our polished wood floor without help. He nodded a hello and forced himself forward.

He'd gained all his weight back and more. His chin and jaw line had admitted defeat, buried under a layer of fat and stretched, drooping skin. No neck was visible anymore just his head rising out from shoulders flecked with small pieces of skin from the psoriasis on his scalp. He lumbered forward, stopped again, panted, and slowly scoped the room. He looked worse than I'd ever seen him.

In came his new wife Vikki, carrying a large

white bakery box, her blond feathered hair flashing brightly in the dim hallway. She grinned me a hello, the few teeth on her top row all askew, big dark pockets between them. She moved in to give me a brief hug and a "How ya been Josh?" and "Good, good". In came her two sons. They were thirteen and six; the younger one was my dad's. They whispered hi, uncertain eyes scanning the room for something familiar. My wife, Pam told them we had a backyard and they ran past me and my sisters out through the sliding doors where my younger and much smaller sons were racing around.

My California cousins were on their way over for our first New York reunion in years. We hadn't seen each other since we all started having babies. When my cousins came to town most of my family came out of the woodwork, everybody but our oldest brother, Jake, who none of us had heard from since my wedding five years ago. And of course, Dad.

My sister Rachel wanted me to invite him since he hadn't returned her phone calls. I didn't know why she asked me this; he was the one who had kicked me out of the house all those years ago. I hadn't heard anything from him since Pam and I took the boys to visit him in the hospital when he was there a year and half ago, just after we had Ben.

It was unlikely that Dad would actually make it

out of Brooklyn; he never went anywhere, especially since the cancer. But none of us knew how he was doing so I left him a message and here he was. Miraculous.

"Your house is so beautiful. So big." Vikki still had her black jacket with the Pepto Bismol pink sleeves zipped up to her neck in the warm room but she went over to Dad and helped him take his jacket off.

"Did you give them the dessert?" he asked her. "We brought you a cheesecake sampler from Cheesecake Queen."

"Yeah, three different flavors," Vicki said.

Dad's watered down blue eyes made their way to me, and then to Pam. He slowly reached his left hand out to paint the picture; his voice was soft, but bursting with suspense. "They have chocolate mousse cheesecake, carrot cake cheesecake, what's that other one…"

"Kahlua, you mean the Kahlua," Vikki said over her shoulder and wandered over closer to Pam, whose hair was pulled back into a damp ponytail, fresh from a fast shower. She smiled at Pam who was setting our long dining room table with all the salads and appetizers she had asked me to get at the Key Food that morning. She smiled back at Vikki but didn't move from behind the table.

Vikki gave her the bakery box. A large leather Marilyn Monroe winked at me from the back of

Vikki's jacket. She took in all the deli containers and the greasy white wrapping paper the lox had come in.

"I didn't know they have deli out here too!" she said, happy to have learned something new. I caught Pam's eyes fluttering momentarily at the notion that tuna salad, knishes, and lox had never made it out of Brooklyn.

"Yeah," Pam said and smiled back; eyebrows raised a little bit in disbelief.

We didn't know Vikki well. Pam had met her for the first time at our wedding. She spent most of the night sipping vodka cranberries in a shiny blue dress, twirling around my dad's chair like a dizzy planet. Dad was her man, a father for her boys. And since he'd gotten sick, the only person Dad let in his life.

None of us kids really had a sense of what was happening with him. When my sisters and I saw each other we'd piece together a scrap or two of news about his health, shake our heads, and then move on. Rachel, and my younger sister, Sarah, and her family made the three-hour drive from Pennsylvania and slept over last night. We all woke up early, sitting around our coffee in pajamas, noshing, playing with the kids. My boys hardly ate; they were running through the house laughing hysterically trying to escape their uncle who chased them, calling, "The tickle birds are coming!"

Pam spent all of breakfast cuddling Sarah's

baby in her lap; throughout the meal she looked from the baby and then back to me a "so, how 'bout it?" on her face.

Another baby. I just shook my head. The thought of another little one so completely dependent on Pam and me was almost too much to take. At three and a half and one and a half, Jon and Ben had only started to seem less helpless. If I let myself think about how much they need us, my chest gets tight, I can't stand how they could hurt. Maybe when they're bigger I won't worry about them in the same way. They'll have more protection from the world and the things that happen when you least expect it. How people you love can let you down.

The doorbell rang, as promised, at 11:00 sharp, and our cousins and their kids spilled into the house, loudly, clamoring to see and to hug everybody. They patted Dad's back gently and asked how he was. The room overflowed all at once with bodies and suitcases and presents for the kids. They must have taken twenty pictures of Sarah's baby before I got them to take their jackets off. I piled them up on the back of the sofa while Pam handed out coffees.

The cousins loved the house. It was more space than any of us had growing up and they couldn't get over it, all I'd accomplished. How I had straightened up after all the self-destructive stuff I had done when I was little, ditching school, stealing cars, doing whatever I wanted because there was nobody actually raising me.

We all milled around, catching up, drifting closer to the chairs I had scattered around the dining room table. Pam put out a large plate of sliced bagels. Dad had grabbed the back of an upholstered chair for support and was resting when Ben toddled in from the backyard into the dining room, and halted right in front of him. Vikki looked over at him with an ecstatic "Oh, hi baby!"

"Who's this? Is that Ben?" Dad asked.

"Yeah, that's him." Vikki said.

Dad's lips migrated to the right in a quarter smile. "You remember me?"

Ben stared back at the massive man.

"Here," Dad's bloated fingers groped around for something in the front pocket of his shirt. "I got something for you." After another thirty seconds of digging he pulled out a small orange marble and held it out. "You can have it."

Ben stared at the marble. He looked back up at Dad. Then he grabbed the marble and popped it in his mouth.

Pam dropped the forks she was holding and made it over to Ben just before I did. In one motion, she scooped Ben up over her knee and swept the marble out of his mouth. When she had him upright she told him, "That's not for eating."

And then she took his hoodie off and kissed his fuzzy blond head and held him. He hid his face in her shoulder and snuggled in tight.

Dad stood watching, Vikki moved over to Ben. "You okay, baby?" Her arms were outstretched, to squeeze his arm, pat his head, hug him, something. But just before her big hands, with rings screwed tight on every finger, made contact, she must have noticed how little of his body was actually available with his mother holding him, breathing him in. Her hands stopped short at the last minute and found each other in a nervous clasp.

Vikki went back over to Dad. "He's a real cutie," she said and then she fiddled with the zipper to her jacket.

"Did you show them your jacket?" Dad asked. She told us it was new, that Dad had gotten it for her.

"Yeah, I surprised her with it." he explained. A light flickered across his face for a moment, his tired eyes a little brighter with pride.

Dad used to like to surprise us, too. When we were little, before Mom and Dad got divorced, he would bring home little animals. We had kittens, puppies, and, at Easter time for some reason, even though we were Jewish, Dad would get us ducklings or baby rabbits.

He would walk into the house carrying a cardboard box with air holes punched in it, and the four of us kids would swarm him, Rachel and Sarah shrieking with excitement, our oldest brother Jake's rigid arm pushing us out of the way to try to get to the box first.

"All right little monsters, back off a minute," Dad would say and he'd sit in his big chair in our dim living room and tell us to quiet down, cause we were gonna give the animals a heart attack. So we'd sit around him, shifting our weight from knee to knee while we waited, anxiously searching for a nose or paw to poke through a hole, a clue to end the suspense that was nearly killing us. Waiting like that together, we were free; our eyes grew big enough to hold everything, Dad, each other, possibility, happiness. In that moment, there was no room for anything else.

Then Dad would open the box and pick up whoever was huddled down there in the dark and hold it up by him, petting it. When we were truly quiet he'd hand the animal, warm and smelling of stale newspaper from the bottom of the box, over to one of us to snuggle first. It was theirs. The rest of us would whine and edge in closer to get a turn.

"Feed and water it, don't forget," Dad would say and then he'd sit back in his chair, his eyes twinkling a little bit, satisfied. We'd stay in the living room near Dad's chair fawning over our new pet, we wouldn't move from the spot. Dad would shout an occasional "Be careful!" as we pawed those small shaking animals with their big, trembling eyes.

Most of them were replacement pets Dad kept bringing home. I don't remember what happened to all of them. They would be there and then they wouldn't. We should have had dozens of animals roaming the house but they never lasted that long. They'd wander away or get hurt, disappear. We should have taken better care of them, but I guess we didn't know how. The grown-ups didn't either.

Dad had made it to the living room. He was almost sitting in our big recliner, his hands clutched the armrests, engulfing them; his knuckles were white with the effort of lowering his 350-pound mass gently. At the very end he hovered, not sure if he could make the last bit gradually, or if he should call it a day and freefall the last inch to the seat. Sarah, exhausted from another night of interrupted sleep, her baby boy on her hip, moved over to Dad to help in some way but wasn't sure how. Vikki was there now, too, and she moved the corduroy throw pillow off the seat for him. As his body came to a rest, completely filling all the empty space in the chair, a rush of air from his effort flooded through his body. When it rose to somewhere between his nose and throat, he pressed his lips together hard, forcing it back where his throat suffocated it like air out of a tire. His soft, big body deflated.

Sarah leaned on the armrest of the sofa, near

Dad, her thin pretty face pinched, her big blue storybook eyes troubled. She patted his faded green and white flannel sleeved arm for a second and searched him, like I think all of us kids did, for recognition.

It was like that with Dad for all of us except for Jake, who lived in Indiana now. He had a little girl that he took care of on weekends. None of us had seen him in years. He had always been a little off, violent, especially after our parents' divorce. My mom, after several years of trying, could only handle my two sisters. Dad took custody of Jake and me.

Dad seemed to understand Jake. They had the same unpredictable anger and sudden deadness in their eyes when they were going to turn, like a shifty housecat who, sick of being touched, suddenly sinks its teeth into your hand and won't let go.

It was because of Jake that Dad kicked me out when I was twelve. Over a car phone. Jake had been getting into gang fights in Brooklyn, stealing cars and selling them. He took anything he could get his hands on. When he and his asshole friend swiped a phone from the limousine Dad drove, he lied and blamed me.

I came home from school eating a slice of pizza I'd picked up at Al Dente's, and out of nowhere, there was Dad, his uncombed hair sticking out at the sides, not dressed for work yet and loud, asking me if I thought I was so smart.

Trouble.

I wasn't sure if he was talking about me cutting school on Monday or the ten dollars I took from the wad of bills in his room, but I wasn't copping to either. He was close to me and I saw no room in his eyes, no window.

"What?" I said back, irritated and a little jumpy.

His lips curled around his top teeth and he got louder. "You steal from me like some smart ass hood?"

I told him I didn't know what he was taking about and lifted up my slice as casually as I could to take a bite. He knocked the pizza out of my hand before I could rip off a piece.

My face felt hot and huge but my body seemed to shrink. Back then he was six foot two and fifty pounds overweight, most of it in his gut.

His fist winded up and he told me if I didn't tell him the truth I was going to get it, so help him. I ran to the kitchen. He grabbed my arm and shoved me into the wall and told me that he knew I took the phone from the limousine.

"You lying sack of shit, I let you live here and feed you and you steal like some hood."

"What, I didn't!" I hollered back.

"You took my car phone you little shit!"

"I didn't—"

He pinned me against the chalky wall, more

gray now than white from all the grubby handprints. Dad's whole face and neck and chest had turned from whiter than his old undershirt to bright pink. On his left wrist I saw the Rolex watch glinting gold right next to my face and decided, once and for all, that he had gotten it hot.

The front door opened. Jake came in with his best buddy. Still pressed against the wall, I looked over at him for help. Jake had to have seen that. He looked at Dad and then he looked at me. He looked at his friend and said "Oh shit!" and they left. I heard the door slam and their big feet clomping down the stairs. My insides felt like they had been sucked out. I forced myself to turn back to Dad's red glare and pushed back.

"It wasn't me!"

He shoved me harder and held me there. He was a flash of gold and pink and teeth. I closed my eyes; my stomach heaved waves of heat. He'd never hit me but I'd never seen him this out of control. Finally, not too hard, I kicked him in the shin.

He lost his grip to reach for his leg. "Son of a bitch!"

I ran out of there and hid in the hallway watching, ready to bolt.

It was quiet.

I saw him go into my room. He opened my dresser drawer and started throwing socks and underwear out into the living room. Then he opened my closet, grabbed an armful of hangers and swung them out of the bedroom. I heard plastic and metal clanking and then landing with a thud on nubby brown carpet.

"Out. Out of my house!"

And when I asked where I was supposed to go he told me he didn't care, I could call my mother, just get out. Even when I begged to stay, he only stood in the doorframe to watch me pack. His eyes never looked me in the face. I stuffed as many of my things as I could into two shiny Hefty bags, the whole time waiting for him to change his mind.

I spent that night at Scotty's house. I lived there for months, his parents made a room for me, his mother fed me and his father took me wherever Scotty went. We were like brothers. His family made sure I was safe until another friend's folks in the neighborhood could put me up. I lived like that for years.

My mom would come out from Queens after work sometimes to find me so she could bring me back to live with her and my sisters. I always hid. She would sit and cry on the front stoop of my Dad's run-down apartment building and wait for me not understanding why I ran away from her. But I couldn't live out there with her, I'd go out of my mind. I was better off in Brooklyn, looking out for myself. That's when I started stealing cars.

Me and Scotty and some guys from the neighborhood would jack these cars, run them out on the Major Deegan as fast as we could and then hack them for parts. Twelve, thirteen years old and we went from car to car, taking whatever we could, laughing about it the whole time. We did whatever we wanted, drank, cut school, stayed out all night. We were out of control. My future was so far from good that I did everything I could to make it worse.

I don't know how I survived all that, how I made it out of my early life. Somewhere inside I guess I knew I wanted to get out and be safe. I wanted to be good again. My friends, they laughed at me when I told them I was going to go to college someday. But then I did it. I straightened out. I got back to who I was before I had to start fighting to make it. That's when I met Pam. She changed everything for me.

It was noon and everybody was on their second helpings. Pam's warm hand was on my shoulder, a gentle squeeze. She put a plate in front of me though she knew I wouldn't be able to eat much today. The dining room was bursting with overlapping voices. When one person spoke, everybody craned their necks to hear and listened just long enough to take over the conversation.

Dad and I hadn't said much since he arrived. Now that he was here, I wasn't sure any more why he had made the effort, for me and my sisters, or to see his nieces and nephews.

We never talked about it, my sisters and I. I guess we just took what we could get and put it away, saved to pick through and wonder about later. Any settled feelings we had about Dad drummed inside us weakly, in fits and starts, never picking up any real rhythm. But still, I wanted to know what he thought of the house or about the boys. Maybe this time he would find a way to make things better.

Vikki brought another plate over for Dad. He had been sitting motionless in the living room, his arms holding onto the armrests like he came with the chair, like he was growing out of it. He couldn't move his head around much either. While Sarah talked, he raised only his eyes to her and it gave him an odd look of deference. Knowing her time would be up at any minute, she was getting in what she could in the practiced, unimposing way she had used to survive growing up, unnoticed, as the baby of the family, the last child. How was his health, how did he feel, how's things?

Then came Rachel. She pulled a chair up right in front of Dad when she saw he was giving audience, though had he been able to move, he might not have stayed for a round with his other daughter. She tilted her head coyly, and smiled. She was reminding him about that time he drove us into the City to see the tree at Rockefeller Center in his work car and left us there so he could do a job. "I was so little, and you put me in charge!" beaming to reminisce about something she didn't even remember herself. Mom had told her about this once and Rachel held onto it, and told it as best she could, not understanding it was not a good story. She basked in the glow; misunderstanding occasional eye contact for interest; like a bit player with a brief walk-on who thinks the audience is giving them the standing ovation.

Pam had called all the boys in and they tumbled over to plates she had made for them. We were all in the room except for Ben, who was napping.

As if on cue, Rachel asked, "Dad, have you talked to Jake?"

"Yeah," Dad said to his plate while he organized his next forkful.

"How is he?"

"He's doing all right," he said and took a bite of chopped liver.

While she swallowed, Vikki waved her hand out in front of her as placeholder, and then chimed in.

"He's devoted to Kristy. She's his life."

Dad looked up. "Yeah, he's a great father."

Pam stopped her fork on its way to Jon who was trying to flatten himself into his chair back and then duck in the hopes of escaping another bite. Her eyes came to rest on Dad for the first time all morning. Her lips were a hard line.

"Is that right?" she asked.

"Yeah, he just threw her a big birthday party," Vikki went on.

"I'd never seen so many presents for one little kid," Dad said.

I pushed the sweatshirt sleeves up on each of my arms and tapped my glasses higher on my nose. I cleared the gravel from my throat.

"You went out there, Dad?"

"Yeah, last month, we drove out."

"To Indiana?"

"Yeah."

Pam left the room and began clattering dishes in the kitchen and I followed her. She shook her head when she saw me, her hand a question as she gestured toward the dining room.

"What is wrong with him?"

"Classic," I said.

"Why does he do this?"

"He's Dad…"

"I swear I'm going to say something."

"It's not worth it," I said dropping plates into the sink.

"So he can do whatever he wants no matter how it hurts people?"

"He doesn't get it."

"What if he does though?"

I leaned on the counter. Through the kitchen window I watched two crows hop on the lawn. "He's not going to change."

She moved her hand to my cheek and held it

there for a moment.

"It's okay. I'll be okay."

"You don't have to be," she said searching my eyes.

"I know," I said holding her. "I can't talk about it now." I kissed her hand and picked up a fruit platter to take to the dining room.

When we finished brunch everybody poured into the backyard; it was unseasonably warm out for November and we sat in the teasing sun.

My Dad had made the thirty feet to the patio in record time. His lumbering journey was interrupted with stifled groans that started deep inside from where the cancer had set up shop in his bladder and in his prostate. His eyes glazed over in pain every time his feet or ankles made new contact with the ground or pressed against his sneakers. I pulled the nearest cushioned patio seat out for him and wondered if the cancer cells were re-amassing in the space where one of his kidneys had been removed. If they were strategizing their attack on that organ's sadly unsuspecting twin.

The kids chased each other and swung and lay on the hammock, different relatives took turns pushing them. Ben woke up from his nap and I brought him outside. He smiled dreamily, squinting in the late afternoon glare, and Rachel took him from me to cuddle. I moved over to the cousins. We talked about how good it was to see each other, how there was never enough time, and would they ever consider moving back east. It was the same every reunion.

When I checked back on Ben, Rachel had put him in Dad's arms. She smiled encouragingly at me when she saw that I had noticed.

Ben was still not totally awake yet, his eyes were hazy, and his cheek was glued to his grandpa's shoulder, his body turned toward him, koala style. Dad's big arms held him and the two of them rested, peaceful together, though Dad seemed a bit surprised to have Ben in his arms. Like out of the blue, some little boy had just fallen out of the sky and stuck to him. I stayed put and watched Dad with him. He looked down every few minutes to check that Ben was still there, bewildered amusement dancing in his eyes a little each time. I didn't know Dad had the patience to hold anyone that long. I had no memory of anything like that.

Pam brought out fresh hot coffee and Vikki handed Dad a cup. My cousins brought out their cameras again, to capture what they saw. Here was their uncle: big, ill, and older than they remembered, holding his sweet, cuddly pint-sized grandson. Rachel took pictures. Everybody took pictures. For a moment, I could see what my cousins must have seen gathered around with their cameras, the beautiful certainty of a grandfather and his grandchild.

Pam cut the cheesecake. Ben still lay on Dad's

chest as the last of the cameras were put down and people settled into their chairs. I was in the kitchen, a plate of cheesecake in each hand, waiting for Pam to right a piece that had toppled over, when I heard the first cries. I looked out and saw Dad's hot coffee cup lifted high in one hand, his other hand still on Ben's back, but poised in surprise. Coffee dripped from both the coffee cup and Ben. He was still stuck to Dad, but screaming, steam billowed from his face and head.

Oh my gods ricocheted in rounds off the patio but nobody moved. If Dad felt panic, it was unreadable. It was locked up in his sick swollen body. He was trapped, heavy in his chair with Ben lying on him and crying desperately. Dad managed to keep his coffee cup still with his one hand, while his other hand, the one on Ben, slowly lifted up and reached out for help.

Pam rushed out with "what happened" and then "oh my god." I ran out after her and grabbed him from Dad.

I heard him stammer, "I, I didn't know he was going t-to turn his head. I was taking a sip and he, it spilled…"

"Put him in the bath," Pam shouted and we ran the water ice cold. We poured it over the light pink marks on Ben's forehead and left cheek. He cried and shook his head. I shushed him and held his head still. Every time we poured water on him, he screamed again, and then grabbed at my shoulders to get away from the water and the raw feeling of his skin.

I scanned Ben's face. His skin wasn't broken. I lifted him out of the tub to hold him. He sobbed and hiccupped.

"It's going to be all right, my boy," I said softly, my heart thumping hard.

He was more scared than badly injured. I hugged him to me as I put him in the big towel Pam was holding open. She sat on the edge of the tub with Ben wrapped up tightly in her arms. He turned away, into her chest. She kissed him and patted his back. He sniffled, quieting.

Pam looked up at me, her eyes small, serious. "What was he doing holding him anyway? He's only seen him twice in his life!"

From the hallway there was a heavy shuffle. I heard Dad smother a groan. He looked over into the bright bathroom, his brows meeting in a worried peak. He leaned into the wall, resting his shoulder on it for support. There were tiny drops of sweat on his crown and over his top lip.

Still panting a little bit from his walk, he looked at me. "How's he doin', Josh?"

Pam was watching me. Ben was calm in her arms.

"I didn't mean to…" he said. "I feel bad."

I could hear it. His voice was gentle, like it had been when I was little and home sick or when he'd tell me a story and watch my reaction.

I used to think about that softness in his voice and what I had done to make it go away. It was the sound of the dad he could be if he loved me enough or remembered me. Who for so long I wanted to believe might still be in there.

The dad I realized even now part of me had been holding out for, maybe like all children do. Even grown up ones who should know better.

He stood facing the three of us and his lip twitched. Like he was about to say more.

I wanted to make it easier for him the way I always have. But I wouldn't let myself. I waited for him to go on.

He glanced at me again. But his eyes drifted away. And then he turned around. My chest tight, I watched him make his way slowly back down the hall.

I know he won't ever be able to do better when it comes to me. That doesn't stop it from hurting. From feeling like we've lost something again each time.

Rick's Wax Hands

I left Rick at the fair and my heart won't stop going fast. My body was shaking but I walked away, through the wind, out past the field. I didn't turn around. Outside the storm is still whipping all the trees around, the branches jerk and swirl like wild tentacles. It's getting dark in my room and he still hasn't come for me.

The storm started just an hour after we opened today. I had nine people standing in line when wrappers and used napkins from the garbage cans blew past our display table. But Rick was already in a bad mood, even before the weather turned. I could tell by the way he shoved my flowers to the side of the table when we set up.

When Rick's in a bad mood he stares at me with this look while we work and I'll know I've done something to upset him. He might not say anything the whole rest of the day. When he's upset he goes far away inside and there's nothing I can do to bring him back until he's ready. Some-times he drops me off at my place and drives off to his house. I can't sleep those nights. Rick's all I have anymore.

I know that I know how to stake that canopy. I've been doing it since Rick first said I could help him. He says fifty-five-year-olds aren't girlfriends but I'm not his wife and I'm not his friend so I'm his girlfriend.

After we were together a year I asked him why not let me manage the customers waiting in line. He thought about it over winter and then he said I could give it a try. I hugged him for so long when he told me. I promised I would never miss a fair, no matter what; I would always be there to help him.

This is how it goes when we work: I stake the four "Rick's Wax Hands" canopy poles and then I set out the wax hand displays by price. Rick goes and has his coffee and cigarette and focuses for the day because he's the artist. No wax hand artist in the whole Pacific Northwest can do what Rick does. That's what he told me when I first met him and it's true.

He can dip all kinds of people's hands into the paraffin; from crying babies to adults. Even couples while they hold each other's hands. He wraps his fingers around their wrists and guides them down into the warmed vat. And then he pulls them out of the gray white wax, smooth and dripping and perfect. When they harden up a little, it's time to slide the new hollow hand off the real one. They are as fragile as newborns and Rick is so gentle with them. I stop breathing a little each time he slips a new wax skin off somebody's hand and dips them in vats of color.

Today, just before everything happened I was talking to a couple about the double dip. Their three kids were waiting with an old man across the path, stuffing handfuls of kettle corn into their mouths. They all kept looking up at the canopy. I followed their eyes and saw the green canvas rippling, the poles kind of swaying. I tapped Rick on the back but he said not now, he was starting a dip.

"Excuse me, ma'am," said the next man on line, a farmer it looked like. He asked if it was extra to get three colors on his hands, he was surprising his wife for her birthday. I said not at all, he could get up to four colors. When I spoke, I could see him listening to me, like it was important. He looked at my eyes in this steady way the whole time.

And then I saw half of the canopy sink behind him. The other side tilted forward and it was as if the whole thing was coming for me, like in a dream. It felt almost like the ground was rising up beneath me because of how close I was suddenly to it. And then it collapsed.

The first corner of it landed in the paraffin vat. Then the second pole buckled and the rest of the canopy fell crashing onto the wax display table. I was still watching Rick's stuff fly everywhere when the second metal pole hit the farmer on his head.

I saw how red Rick's face was when everything got crushed and my heart was racing. I thought all these things at once: "the hands—the wax—Rick—that farmer." But the farmer was holding his head; I rushed to him right away. I put my hand on his back and I asked him if he was okay. He stood there rubbing his head and staring at the ground. He didn't answer.

I looked over to Rick for help. He wagged his pinky finger with the ring on it to call me over. I rescued a wax thumbs-up-hand and a peace-sign-hand from the ground on the way. Things were a mess, but that didn't mean every-thing was ruined.

"Look, these two are still in good shape."

But Rick wouldn't look back at my eyes; he set the wax hands down and we worked on one of the fallen poles. As we drove it back into the wet ground, he kept his eye on the people walking on the path. He stretched his mouth into a stiff smile only if somebody turned to watch us. When the pole was back in the dirt again, I put my hand on Rick's arm. He jerked it away.

"Go back over to that guy with the head and apologize."

"Oh, I did."

"No Joyce, listen to me very carefully. Can you do that?" His breath smelled like his last cigarette and Certs.

"Tell him *you* didn't follow instructions when you

set up the canopy. Tell him that you are very sorry and that it's your fault."

"But, honey, I staked those poles like always. Like always."

"I am not going to get sued for some concussion because you can't do anything right."

The wind was gusting and two of the couple's kids were crying but they still wanted a double dip so Rick turned back to them.

I brought the man with the hurt head my resting stool for him to sit and I told him what Rick had said to say. I picked up the other fallen pole to re-stake it. But it was wet from the rain, and I couldn't get it to stay in the ground by myself.

"Ma'am, why on earth are you the one staking the canopy?" the man asked.

I stared at him. I was thinking of an answer when he got up and walked over to Rick.

Rick was holding the couple's hands together over the paraffin vat. That's when the man with the hurt head asked Rick for his business card and Rick, without turning his face to him, told him he didn't know what had happened to them in the storm.

"Well, I need you to find me one." The man said again.

"I don't know what to tell you. I'm out."

They talked loudly. The man asked for Rick's phone number and through clamped teeth Rick said he could get that at the grounds office if it was so important to him. The man turned away from Rick.

He came over to me and spoke in this quiet way, his deep-set blue eyes on my face.

"What's this guy's last name?"

"Evans."

"Where you all live at?"

"Fall City."

"I'll be in touch. Thanks, lady."

I just answered. The way he talked to me made me feel different from myself. I watched him walk toward the office, near the entrance to the fair.

The leaves on the trees around us were fluttering, wet and shiny like dark cellophane. Candy wrappers blew out of a garbage can and past my feet.

That's when I saw it. The smallest cracked orange wax hand from a toddler lying on the ground. The stubby fingers reaching out, one fingertip missing. I couldn't leave it lying there that way.

I felt Rick watching me when I bent down to pick it up. He was shaking his head as I stood up. He flipped and flipped his hair off his forehead with his pinky finger, but the wind kept blowing it back into his eyes.

He looked at me like I was a dog. "Hey Joyce!"

My heart stopped for a second when I heard him. Then he said, "I have an idea, Joyce." I pulled my black sequined cardigan around me tighter, tried to smile.

His mouth twisted and his eyes turned narrow and he screamed, "WHY DON'T YOU FIND SOME-BODY ELSE'S LIFE TO RUIN?"

I felt my lip trembling. I couldn't make it stop. I wished the canopy would collapse again so Rick would stop yelling. I felt the smoothness of the toddler hand in mine and I pressed my fingertips against it.

I couldn't look at Rick staring at me like that. I had to turn away. I reached under the tablecloth for my purse. And then I started walking. I walked all the way to the parking lot. There weren't many cars left and I could see clear across the dirt field to Rick's car. I rode with him this morning.

I stood there holding the toddler hand. It was cold outside and I couldn't hold the hand carefully and keep my sweater from blowing wide open. But I didn't want to drop it into my purse, it would get crushed.

The couple passed by, and in the husband's cupped hands I could see their clasped wax hands, dipped in red, white, and blue. Their three kids and the old man trailed behind. The toddler was still crying, snot shone on her lip. The mom jammed her into a car seat with quick, hard movements, and slammed the door to their old truck. I watched their taillights as they left the parking lot.

And then I started to walk again. I walked with my head down against the wind until I was out of the field. I kept going until I got to a gas station.

I found a trucker there and he let me sit in the cab out of the wind while he gassed up. I watched the road for Rick's car. I saw a woman in a short violet coat leave the gas station with her daughter. She was holding a coffee cup in each hand but when the little girl stopped, she stopped also and bent down to talk to her. With her eyebrows raised and her chin tucked to her chest, she explained something to the pony-tailed girl in a patient way. The little girl looked up, her mouth open a little while she listened and then she held on to the end of her mother's jacket and they crossed the rest of the way.

If my daughter had grown up, I would have tried to be like that mom in the violet coat, patient and calm. My baby would have known I loved her. Maybe I'm still punishing myself, loving Rick. But, it hardly matters, I have lost that, too. I have lost everything.

It's dark now. No matter where I sit the draft from outside comes in through the cracks of my bedroom window and finds me. I can feel a cold pinprick of air drilling into my cheek, my forehead. And the rushing wind sounds won't stop building up and settling down, building up and settling down. Then it's quiet, quieter than before it even started. It's so quiet I think it will break me open.

I haven't left the bedroom window in hours. The moon has moved up far away. It's tiny and cold in the sky. I can hardly make out the little orange hand I'm holding, but I can feel it. Each section of each tiny finger. I close my hand into a fist around the little wax fingers. I don't want to cry anymore. I press against the soft wax and it gives. I squeeze and my fingertips move closer to the edge of my palm. I press and squeeze and I feel a wax finger fold into itself. Then another finger folds. The middle caves in like an ice cream cone. The space inside my hand changes and my own fingertips meet my palm. My hand closes completely, as if there is nothing at all inside it.

It is almost morning; there are no cars on the road. I carry the balled hand just outside the front door and see some of my daisies still blooming in the cold. I choose one that still has all its orange petals and I bury the softened wax beside it.

I'm not waiting anymore.

What February
Feels Like

B y the time I leave for the bus to work, the raised
white bumps spelling out "Housatonic River" on
the green highway sign are starting to reflect passing
headlights. The poor river always looks so cold in
February, rushing past with all its noise and splash. It
still has PCBs in it from the GE plant that was here
thirty years ago. So sad that a beautiful thing like that
can't actually be what it seems.

My dad and I used to go down and watch the river
a lot when my mom first brought me here to live with
him. She was supposed to come up to Pittsfield from
Virginia tonight for my birthday weekend. Sweet
sixteen, that's me.

She hasn't visited since last summer. My stomach was nervous butterflies all week just thinking about it; I could hardly eat and the last two nights I didn't sleep well. After school today, I practically ran home. I had almost finished straightening up the apartment for her when she called and cancelled. Work or something. I felt little prickles around my head when she told me. My throat went tight and I could barely speak—I had to move to the window for some air. "Take care of yourself," she said before she hung up.

I stood there holding the phone, looking out from the third floor window. I stared at the naked trees reaching up for the sky with their vein-like branches, I smelled chimney smoke from one of the houses down the street. My forehead was pressed against the icy glass when Botchnik's called to see if I could fill in, they were down a server. I asked if Rob was working and they said yes he was.

That's when I decided tonight is the night.

I'm not going to spend my whole birthday weekend sitting around this dumb town thinking about how much better everything would be if Mom were here. It hurts too much. She can do whatever she wants, it doesn't matter to me anymore. I'm going to make things better for myself.

Tonight, I'm going to ask Rob for a ride home and I'm going to kiss him. And when he kisses me back it will feel like we're melting in the dark together. He'll put his arms around me and press me to his chest and we'll stay that way. He won't want to let me go.

The sun is almost gone by the time my bus comes. Dad likes me to sit near the bus driver, he's been telling me that since I was ten, when Mom first dumped me up here. That first summer Dad let me paint my bedroom bright pink and he took me to a ton of garage sales. We walked to the diner every weekend and we talked about all kinds of stuff. We don't anymore. Maybe it got hard for him to pretend all the time that we were fine. That we both weren't wishing my mom would change her mind and come back.

When I get on the bus it smells like heat and old bodies. I pass two crepe-y ladies on my way to the back. I don't care what my father says, I can sit wherever I want. I'm going to be sixteen tomorrow.

I'm still not sure why me and Ruby are allowed to serve liquor at Botchnik's; I think everybody thinks we're eighteen. Dad knows but doesn't seem bothered by it, it's only twice a month. He says I have a good head on my shoulders and twelve dollars an hour off the books is twelve dollars an hour I won't need to ask him for.

Ruby is the one who got me the job, and Ruby knows about the world. She and her boyfriend have done it. I asked her about it and she told me it's like feeling pressure up inside, near your stomach. I can't imagine it, I mean, she is sixteen-and-a-half, but still. Ruby gets to live with her mother and her mother smokes cigarettes and boils frozen Contadina ravioli and puts red sauce on it and Ruby has her boyfriend over and they all eat dinner like a family.

Rob has a huge dinner every Sunday after church with his entire family. They all still live in Pittsfield and sometimes Rob makes the Sunday meal for everyone. He wants to go to school to be a chef; he's only bartending to make money. He was fourteen when he cooked his first meal for everyone and this is something he told me in confidence and when he did I didn't say a word, not until I was sure he was finished because I knew how special it was that he was telling me. He told me it was going to be Lamb Kebab Night but when Rob went to the butcher shop, and saw a whole lamb lying on the counter, he got so upset he had to leave. He just couldn't do it. So he made vegetable kebabs for his family that night instead and his brothers still make lamb noises and razz him about it sometimes.

I step off the bus and walk the block to Botchnik's. Whenever I work with Rob I have a good time. He always gets me my cocktails first and he's been teaching me how to do the garnishes. We talk about the guests at the parties—I told him it seems to me everybody drinks like it's their last night on earth. Rob says the alcohol helps them feel better about themselves.

When he gets really busy, he can barely look up at me when I come to the bar, but this smile sometimes shows up on the side of his face and I can tell I've made him laugh or at least I'm not annoying him. He never laughs at anybody else at work like that. I feel like a real person around him. He's twenty-three.

When I open the heavy wood door a damp saltine smell comes from the trampled carpet. Faded leafy tendrils swirl over threadbare maroon fabric that I am sure has been there for at least fifty years. Rob is behind the bar when I walk in, wearing his white shirt and black vest. I check to see if he noticed me but he's just looking down, drying wine glasses.

I go straight to the back and flip through the rack of ruffled button-down white shirts to find a size that's tighter than I usually wear and I pull a black vest off a wire hanger. I usually work in sneakers, but tonight I fish black high heels out of my backpack and check them over. I used a Sharpie before I left the apartment to fill in the scuffmarks and they look pretty good. I don't put on my bow tie yet—I want to leave my shirt open at the top for as long as I can. I fix my stockings and pat down my old black skirt. It has nubs on it from when I dried it too hot. I was supposed to get a new one with my mom this weekend, along with a whole bunch of other stuff, a shopping spree she called it. I wanted to go so much. I wish she'd never promised something like that.

When I'm ready I go back out front. Rob has a handful of freshly cut orange slices in his hand and is cramming them into the garnish caddy for cocktails. I fluff my hair out again and join him at the bar to fill water glasses.

"Hey, you don't want to put the glasses into the ice bucket, remember?" Rob has a smooth face with a high hairline. He probably had more of his dark blond hair even just a year ago, but it was shrinking away from his roundish forehead. He looks up at me with his eyebrows arched. "The glass could break in the ice."

"Oh, yeah. I forgot." I make sure to look into his eyes when he hands me the scooper and I keep on looking. I sneeze.

"Gesundheit. How's the prettiest girl in high school?"

I laugh. "Good I guess. I got third place at the science symposium."

He looks at my blouse where it's unbuttoned. "That's great."

"Oh, I almost forgot to tell you!" I prop myself up on the bar with my elbows. "I was so scared on the ride over here today."

"Why?"

I open my eyes wide and try to look worried. "I thought we were going to crash into a telephone pole."

"What happened?" Rob stops stacking burgundy cocktail napkins. I see him notice my hair.

"We just skidded and skidded all over the place." I whisper this, "I don't think those drivers know what they're doing on the ice." I press a small scotch glass into Rob's stack of napkins so they fan out like rays of a sun. I shake my head still looking down. "It'll be really bad on the way home tonight. You know it's supposed to snow again." My heart is going fast, there's a weird twitch pulling at the left side of my mouth. I bite my lip to stop it. "I bet you're a good driver in the snow."

"Sure." Rob moves over to the garnish caddy. "I'm still alive." He flashes me his smile.

When Mr. Botchnik isn't around, Rob makes snacks for us. He'll pick up a frilly cellophane toothpick, stab some fruit and hand it to me. My favorite is the orange slice, cherry, pineapple combo. He named it The Traci and he gives one to me now. I smile so he knows how special it is to me, and this time, I've never done this before, I touch his finger and thumb when he hands it to me. His skin is cool and smooth. I thank him in my softest voice, I nibble delicately at the large hunk of pineapple, but it's really tough so I end up pulling the whole piece off the toothpick and pop it into my mouth. Rob watches me while I try to swallow it down and then his eyes go off to the left.

"Head's up."

I freeze. Whenever Botchnik comes around, Rob waves his hand to scoot me away, our secret signal that means look busy. I toss the rest of the fruity toothpick behind the bar and scoop ice into my tumblers.

Mr. Botchnik owns the place—he is old and his eyes are always darting behind his thick glasses, like he's looking everywhere for something he lost. His salt and pepper eyebrows dip low over the bridge of his nose and sweep up over his eyes like an enthusiastic checkmark. His legs are really bowed; he looks like a wishbone walking. He never sees me or speaks directly to me; he gives orders in my general direction. I pretty much duck when he comes around.

Tonight he sends me out to the lounge to pass out appetizers. Rob will be at the second bar on the other side of the room.

It's a wedding and there are one hundred and fifty people here, most of them greedily shoving the same hors d'oevres into their mouth like at every event. I have refilled my tray six times in the first half hour. There's pigs in blankets, little spinach pies, vegetarian egg rolls, and chopped liver pâté on melba toasts with curling pieces of dill that are not the fresh forest color of dill, but more like a droopy sage green. I don't touch the stuff. Rob told me when I first worked with him three months ago that all the food at Botchnik's was frozen and recycled and to stay away.

The headwaiter finally opens the doors to the dining room. I wait against the wood paneled wall near the bar and wait for the DJ to ask everybody to sit down so we can serve dinner. I stand first on one foot and then the other—they ache so bad in my high heels.

If my mom had made it up, I'd be sitting on my sofa wearing cozy socks and pajamas by now. I'd drink hot cocoa and she would pour a glass of whatever

Dad had around the house and tell me about who she's dating, like she did the last time I saw her.

I look over at Rob; he's back at his station. I wonder if he thinks about me, I wonder if he knows how I feel.

The guests are seated, I just have one cocktail left to deliver. I'm thirsty and I haven't eaten since lunch. I start for the bar to get some juice. There's a pretty thirty-something woman with neat blond hair in a pompadour talking to Rob. She's wearing a short silver dress and her elbows are on the bar holding a drink close to her mouth. She's got black stockings on and a silver and black purse on a thin chain hanging to her hip. She's leaning over the bar talking to Rob and he's smiling. He's laughing, and in between his quiet looks down at his tumblers and shot glasses, he's looking up at her. He's looking up at her a lot. She's drinking her drink, a White Russian. I know all about White Russians. Rob and I make fun of people who drink them. He says they're just like drinking a milkshake. If I could drink I would have a gin and tonic, that's what Rob drinks. Crisp, clear, serious.

The White Russian lady drains her drink—she and Rob laugh together. He makes her another one and she takes it and sips at it. She's not going anywhere.

I tuck my tray under my arm and walk over to them, trying not to limp from the blister on my big toe; I am as tall as White Russian when I stand up straight.

I flop my tray on the bar. When there's a break in

their laughter I say, "Well, all my tables are eating."

Rob finishes his story, "And that's what they always ask for now."

White Russian giggles and touches his hand. "Who knew vegetable kebabs could bring a family together?"

They laugh again. My cheeks feel hot. Rob told her The Kebab Story.

I take my headband off and run my hands through my hair and fluff it out again, but nobody is watching me. "Hey Rob, can I get something to drink? I'm so hot."

He looks up at me.

I tilt my head to the side and smile.

He winks. "Sure, kiddo."

He called me kiddo. He pours me a club soda and hands it over, no garnish. I look at my drink, which would just be water if it weren't for those bubbles popping around in the tall glass. It is almost not a drink. I reach for a straw and that's when I see it. Rob has a toothpick. He slides a slice of orange on to it, and then a cherry and then a pineapple chunk. He didn't forget after all. He holds it up, spins it around once and then, satisfied, hands it over to White Russian. The Traci. He gave her The Traci. She tucks her chin down low and looks up at him with these big green sparkly eyes and says, "Thank you."

I am sure my eyes are going to pop out of my head if I have to watch anymore. And that's when I do it.

As casually as I can I say, "Oh, I also need two G and Ts."

Rob barely nods at me while he makes the drinks. I watch him work, even though I don't have to—I know his pours, how he drops the lime in casually after he gives it a gentle squeeze. "Here you go."

I lean over as close to Rob as I can get and whisper, "Thanks" right into his ear. I put both drinks on my tray, shoot White Russian a look, and turn. I swing my hips from side to side as I walk away, like a pendulum, the way I see some women do. My shoes slice into the sides of my feet even more this way and I have to suck in my breath. But I keep swinging in case Rob is still watching me.

Finally, I make it to the crowd of paunchy guests who have packed themselves onto the shiny vinyl dance floor. I slip in between them and limp my way across the room as they bob to songs from the eighties.

I get to the lounge all the time pretending to look for the people whose drinks I am carrying. I put the tray down on a gray vinyl chair near the windows and look both ways. I part the beige wool curtains with my shoulder and snatch the two drinks off the tray. I take off my shoes and so nobody will see me hiding, I step on the narrow ledge and press my body against the cold window.

I take my first sip of the first drink. It is icy and bitter and fresh, like a sharp slap in the face. I drink the rest and it cools me. Outside the snow is falling fast. Except for the rubber stamp store sign across the street flickering from dim to dimmer and then dim to dimmer again, all the shops are dark. Only the occasional car passes, lighting up the road. I can hear the faint white noise of tires on snow. I drink up the second drink and imagine the alcohol bathing my insides with its bite, transforming me.

The folds of heavy curtain and the quiet of the dark space are like being at the theatre. After the divorce, when Mom came up to visit that February for my eleventh birthday, she took me to the Colonial Theatre in Boston to see a Broadway style production of *Annie*. The theatre had dark red, freshly vacuumed carpet rolling over everything—it fanned out under every seat, blanketed every step, every rise in the floor. Little tiny lights glowed in peaked bulbs in sconces on ivory walls, and chandeliers hovered like beautiful glass spaceships over our heads. The proscenium, sturdy and sweeping, arched elegantly up in front of us, deep creases cut into its creamy white surface.

The music started loud, booming, and the girls on stage sang with perfect pitch, perfect tilts of their head, and winning little girl smiles. In their perfectly ripped orphan clothing they sang about how hard life was. Their little faces screwed up tight as they romped through the orphanage belting out notes of lament at their unbearable lives. In rags, they jumped from tattered bed to tattered bed and then skidded across the floor on their battered knees in full musical abandon, glowing and happy somehow in their misfortune.

I sat next to Mom wearing my newish dress with

white tights, my feet in patent leather Mary Jane shoes resting on the neat carpet. My mom looked down at me from her program and smiled, happy that I was happy, or happy with herself that she had chosen such a good gift. I craned my neck to see everything. What bliss to be an orphan girl singing about how hard life is, with everyone watching so lovingly.

Annie sang to the audience about her wishes, her pain, but nobody worried too much because we knew nothing bad was going to happen. It was a musical; everything was going to be good in the end. My eyes pulled everything in, crammed every detail into my head.

I wanted to be one of those girls, to be special like that. My mom's perfume wafted over to me in small teasing waves, a reminder she was right there, next to me in the darkened theatre. We were safe and close, the way it was supposed to be. Nothing was better than to sit together like that, included, watching a world where nothing goes wrong.

Even after my mom had driven back to Virginia, I thought about it. But then it just made me sad to remember. If you really can't have something, it's painful to wish for it.

Every part of my body feels weak. My feet are cut up and it burns to put my shoes back on. I come out from behind the curtain and pick up my tray. I've never done anything like this before. I am dizzy. I think I may be drunk. I'm going to find Rob.

It is ten forty-five. The guests finally leave; they

had the DJ play *Celebration* by Kool and the Gang two more times. When I get back to the bar Rob is alone again, loading glasses up on dish racks for the kitchen. I begin to clear glasses off my table on a big tray and carry them back to the bar. I slope left as I walk; my high heels feel like rubber stilts.

All I have to do is ask.

"Where you been, Traci?"

I take tiny careful steps and make it there with all my glasses.

"Everything okay?"

I burp to myself and smile to cover the pause. "Yeah." I set my tray down and take my glasses off one by one. I look at each glass as my hand reaches for it and watch as my hand places it on the bar. Once all the glasses are off my tray, I lean on it. I feel the dampness of the wet cork under my elbows where the glasses left rings. I look up at him, my heavy face in my hands. Here goes.

"Can you drive me home tonight?"

He stops wiping the bar and looks at me. And then he winks. "I think I can do that."

I smile at him like a woman. My insides are fizzing around, and my head feels like a marshmallow. I turn around and somehow make it to another table to load up. The tray is full and ready to pick up now, but I can't imagine having the strength. I slide it out to the edge and hoist it. My hand holding the tray wobbles and the glasses clink together. I cannot walk straight. Rob is still watching me but with a vague look of panic. I take another step forward and my left heel goes out from under me. I am falling, the glasses slide off the tray and orange and brown booze splashes everywhere. The glasses and I hit the floor at the same time. I am surrounded by shards.

It's almost midnight. Small snowflakes are falling steadily as Rob and I drive across town in his black Toyota Corolla. I lean my head against the passenger side window to stop my head from spinning. When Botchnik rushed in red-faced, Rob told him I was sick, that I needed to get home and shushed me so I wouldn't have to explain.

Rob has an air freshener that smells like cedar. I crinkle up my nose and cringe at the cardboard tree dangling from the rearview mirror. "Wood chips."

Rob cranks open all the windows and throws the car freshener onto the road so I won't hurl in his car. "You know, you didn't have to come into work tonight if you didn't want to."

"No," I say, looking at him, "I wanted to work."

"Well, you didn't have to sneak drinks," he says shaking his head.

"I'm sorry."

It's cold in the car with the windows down and the night whipping past us. The windshield wipers go back and forth, but the snowflakes keep coming, shooting down together like stars from the black sky. I watch them, free and falling quickly, as they pile one on top of another. Everything is glittering white and fresh and the air blowing through the car is so clean. I want to believe things can be different but I don't know how to change who I am.

Rob makes a turn and we are driving alongside the river. It rolls by choppy and raw. It keeps moving like it does every day, every night, tumbling past all the apartments, all the houses, with its dirty water but nothing can make it clean again.

Rob pulls onto my street, in front of my building. It is quiet in the car except for the dull knocking of the wind-shield wipers.

"You okay getting in?"

I gather my high heels and backpack from the floor and look at him. "Yeah."

I climb out of the car clutching my bag, my shoes dangle from my fingers. "Thanks, Rob." When I shut the door, a high heel slips out of my fingers and lands on the new snow in front of my building.

I hold on to the rolled down window and lower myself to get it.

I pick up my shoe and shake off the wet snowflakes that have already clumped themselves on the black vinyl.

"Traci?"

"Yeah?"

He gives my hand a squeeze. "Take care of yourself."

I nod and back away from his car.

I'm so tired of taking care of myself.

I walk toward my building. From our third-floor

apartment, blue television light flickers in the window like always when my father is home. My eyes sting. I can't swallow past the lump in my throat. I wipe tears off my face.

Somebody is always missing.

The Plan

Genevieve was on top of the desk again, shouting over the music for people to dial. She ran her fingers through her blond hair and scoped the room like she always did to see whose attention she had. Matthew sat at his cubicle watching her from over his propped-up sales binder—he was still holding his lead sheet but had forgotten who he was dialing the moment Genevieve had climbed up there.

Before Matthew could look away, she met his eyes and slid off the desk. He flipped the pages of his script to the beginning of the pitch and had just finished dialing his next lead when he felt her hands on his shoulders. Her mouth was close to his ear.

"Is tonight the night?"

"I'm working on it."

"Don't work on it," she whispered. "Do it."

Finally, he had her attention. After just six weeks at The Plan he was becoming one of their strongest salespeople. She squeezed his shoulders one more time and walked away, a trace of violet and sandalwood perfuming the air behind her. He refocused on his lead sheets—he only needed to sell three more packages to have the highest sales of anyone for the week.

It was nine fifty-five in Manhattan—only another five minutes before the Team started calling the west coast. JC whipped by and told everybody to focus. His metallic-sheened button-down shirt was soaked at the armpits like it always was by this point in the shift. Thick stubble had erupted over his olive skin, darkening his angular jaw—beads of perspiration clung to his forehead. His real name was Thomas, but they called him JC because the man could sell anything.

Nobody on the Team seemed to know for sure whether Genevieve and JC were still married or not. It was hard for Matthew to understand how they'd ever gotten together. JC was all coiled energy, always ready to spring, but Genevieve was The Plan's creator; she was the content, the draw. The strongest, most dynamic woman Matthew had ever met. She appeared in a room like a shaft of light, transforming the place with her radiance.

Matthew dialed one more lead from the Mountain time zone before it grew too late to call. Across their shared divider Ashley rolled her eyes at something her customer was saying while she finished putting on another coat of mascara. She always came to work in tight dresses and full make-up like she had booked some club gig and was about to go onstage. At nineteen she was the youngest on the Team.

JC streaked by again and pointed at Matthew with his forefinger. "You got one?"

Matthew nodded and JC plugged his headset into the line to listen in.

"I been takin' 'em religiously, I just ain't sure I can keep on."

"Tell her that's what her lesser self wants her to think." JC said.

"Brenda, that's what your lesser self wants you to think."

"Yeah?"

"Tell her continuing when it seems she can't, is what will set her apart."

"You need to keep on, especially when you don't think you can, that's what sets you apart. That's what makes you different."

"Uh huh."

JC rolled his sleeves up around his muscled arms and worked his jaws vigorously around his chewing gum as he listened. He always chomped it as if it was his last piece, like at any moment he expected somebody was going to come and yank it out of his mouth. "You got her, Matty, keep going."

"Anybody can quit, but you decided to make a

change. That's why you do The Plan. That's why you take the supplements." Matthew lowered his voice as he'd been trained. "Let me ask you an important question, Brenda. Do you feel better?"

"I do. Uh huh."

"Are people saying they see a change in you?"

"Sure. Well," she laughed, "I'm also pregnant right now."

"Excuse me, did you say you're pregnant?"

"Un huh."

Matthew muted his headset. "JC, can pregnant women take the supplements?"

"I don't see why not."

Matthew studied JC's gleaming eyes, his sweaty face.

"But, that's a lot of pills, JC."

JC tapped Matthew's script. "Get back to the page, Matty."

Genevieve peered over the divider to hand JC a cup of fresh coffee and he gave her a wink. Matthew turned back to his binder and got to the Objections page.

JC cracked his gum and rolled his eyes. "Let's go Matty: 'I'll tell you what, Brenda...'"

"Brenda, I'll tell you what. I'll tell you what I'll do for you. I'll get you a six-month program for only one hundred and fifty-nine dollars, that way you won't have to worry about reordering for a while."

"I don't know."

"Brenda, you have to reorder now so you don't

have a break in your program. Is the MasterCard we have on file still good?"

"That's a lot of money, I got all these kids."

"This is not about money, Brenda. This is about you. You have people who depend on you to be the best you can be, don't you?"

"Yeah—"

"And the MasterCard is still good?"

"Yes, it is."

"Okay, I'm going to take care of you. I'll also send you The Plan pocket guide for free."

"Well, thank you."

"You are very welcome, Brenda. Take care of yourself, and that baby."

"I will."

JC high-fived him and got up from the desk. He ripped off Matthew's sales sheet and stuck it on the sales peg. "Matty got another one. Who's next?" He went over to Ashley and crouched, his face close to hers, his hand resting on her back, and listened in on her call.

Genevieve came over and dropped a Recharge Vita-Pack pill packet into Matthew's hand. "Here you go, love. JC, can you go help Vincent close? JC?"

JC looked up at Genevieve from where he huddled. "Ashley only has six."

"That's okay." She kept her eyes on him until he got up. "I'll help Ashley."

Ashley looked down and fumbled a few pages in her pitch notebook.

Matthew took off his headset "Genevieve, can I talk to you real quick?"

"Not now, doll. You'll ruin the energy in the room."

"I just had a question about the pills."

"Then meet me in the Studio after you make your next four."

The Focus Studio was also Genevieve's office. When JC and Genevieve weren't in a meeting or having an argument, crashing around in there like Titans, the Team gathered before their shift to listen to Genevieve's Meditations. Afterward the fourteen of them would share something they were grateful for.

Some of the sales team were in their fifties like Sue or had kids, like Vincent or Deborah. They came to the office for the eight to midnight shift after their other full-time jobs. The Team wasn't supposed to discuss their personal lives outside of Grateful Circle, but they did when they could. Deborah had been there since The Plan opened in Manhattan two years ago. She was a single mom and brought her eight-year-old, Owen, in on the nights she had him and he'd do his math and science activity books cross-legged on the faded carpet. That was a special arrangement Genevieve and JC said they'd made for her. They knew Deborah was working The Plan as hard as she could but her Intention wasn't Transformative the way it was supposed to be, which is why she wasn't getting her numbers up.

Most of the Team was younger like Matthew or

Ashley. She had left home at seventeen but ended up in even worse situations: sleeping wherever she could, partying, basically doing whatever it took to keep her from having to go back to her family. It was finding The Plan a year ago that helped her get her act together. Everybody had some story of how they'd made their way here.

For Matthew it had been early May and he'd been facing another go nowhere upstate summer, bracing himself for the deafening cicadas and endlessly empty nights with only the stars to look at, when he called off an ad he'd heard online of Genevieve's voice asking for New York City area Closers—Closers who were ready to change their lives.

Matthew knew of The Plan; he had followed a lot of the principles ever since picking up the book last fall. He had tried to help his mother with it too, had read to her from his copy, but nothing seemed to get her up and out of bed anymore. She wasn't ready to hear what Genevieve taught: You didn't have to accept that what was would always be. Matthew loved that part—just because he grew up a certain way didn't mean he had to have the same life everyone around him did.

He had always been pretty good at sales, whether he was signing students from Cornell and Ithaca up for phone plans, or selling oil changes door to door. He knew he could close; all he needed was the opportunity.

He called the number off the online ad but when

Genevieve told him to come in that afternoon he had stammered, so she hung up on him. He assumed he'd been disconnected; people didn't do that kind of thing where he was from. He dialed her back and when she answered she said there wasn't room at The Plan for people who weren't ready to change their lives Today.

"I am ready to change my life, today," he told her, "I just have to wait until tomorrow to do it. The bus from Elmira gets me into the city at midnight. I can be there first thing in the morning. Are you still there? Hello?"

"We'll see." She'd said and hung up again.

The next morning when Genevieve and JC arrived, Matthew was already there, waiting in front of The Plan's office doors on Lexington, only a little bleary-eyed after his cold shower and long walk across town. They tried him out on a sample pitch and when he closed the sale, they took him on. Just like that, he had Created his own reality. That was The Plan at work: the difference between accidental living and Setting Intention.

Matthew knew The Plan was his best chance at making himself into the person he wanted to be. What he hadn't counted on was how large Genevieve would loom in his days. That *she* would be what he believed. Everything she said sounded inside him like a bell, thrummed within him like a pulse. It was as if she could see inside him. He could feel her picking out the pieces of him that she wanted and he would give them to her.

At eleven-thirty Matthew broke the weekly record with one hundred packages. He felt a surge inside—Genevieve had challenged him to it and he'd done it. He was out of his seat to post his final sale on the board before he had even tossed his headset off.

With the bamboo shades pulled down low in the Focus Studio, and the oscillating fan always circulating the air-conditioned air, you would never know The Plan headquarters was on the basement level of the twenty-story building. The room was painted sky blue with a royal blue velvet sectional nestled in the corner, a burgundy high-backed chair next to it. On the opposite wall a rainbow was painted in fat brushstrokes with a wind chime hanging from a bracket above it so every time the fan blew past the hanging bells, it sounded like a shopkeeper's door had opened.

Deborah's eight-year-old son, Owen, lay sleeping in the hammock hung catty corner between two walls. His hoodie had slipped to the floor and he was curled up small in the cool room, his ribs rising and falling under his T-shirt. Matthew picked up the hoodie and draped it back over Owen.

"Well, well, Matthew. Nicely done." Genevieve said, gliding in and shutting the door behind her.

"I told you I would hit it."

"You did. Hold on a sec, Matthew. Owen, you need to get up." She shook him at the shoulder. "Owen. Go find your mom."

Owen looked up groggily and when his eyes focused, Matthew held the hammock still for him so he could climb out.

"Thanks," Owen said and Matthew handed him his comic book. "Here you go, buddy."

Genevieve opened the door for him and watched him leave.

Owen looked back at her once and then down again at his comic book as he headed for Deborah's cubicle.

"His mother could be sleeping, too, for all the sales she's making," Genevieve said shutting the door. She sat on the edge of her desk facing Matthew where he stood. "Tell me. What's your next goal?"

"I'm about to set it. But I sold a double to a pregnant woman tonight and JC said it was okay."

Genevieve's light eyes were open and clear, but she didn't acknowledge what he'd said.

"And actually, seven of my packages this week are for people who had to give me four different credit cards before one went through for the bargain package."

"And?"

"I'm just wondering, are there some people we shouldn't sell to?"

"Matthew, let me ask you a question." She leaned forward. "Is selling okay with you?"

"Of course it is."

"I don't know. JC and I have invested a lot of time in you. I wasn't going to tell you this yet," she said, lowering her voice and locking eyes with him, "we think—*I* think—you could be a Leader here. But," she shook her head, "maybe you don't want this."

"No, I do. I'm saying I'm just not sure some of these people that are in debt should be on the program right now. Not, for example, if they have children to feed."

"Oh Matthew." She took his hand. "That's your Doubt talking. It means you have more work to do." She brought him to the sofa and swung the Burgundy chair around so she was sitting directly in front of him. "Close your eyes for me. Focus on your breath while you listen to my voice. That's it." She exhaled with him on a count of ten. "There is a reason you reached these people on the phone and there is a reason they talked to *you*.

I want you to remember how you felt when you first came here. You had hope for something better but no way of turning it into something real. Keep your eyes closed, Matthew. See, that's your Doubt again. Relax your forehead. Relax your lips." She ran her fingers lightly down his temple and along his jaw line. "That's it. Let this information in. Let Answers in."

"When you first came here," she continued, her voice vibrating off his cheek, vibrating off his neck, "you weren't sure what it was exactly, you just knew there was something more for you. But some of these people you are calling don't even know there *is* something more. They don't even *have* hope. Remember? You are providing them with hope and you're providing them with the supplements to help them feel their hope come into being. Why would you take away their hope?"

She wrapped her fingers around his left wrist. A shiver pulsed down his spine and traveled through the rest of his body. "I'd like to awaken your Meridians to Consciousness now, Matthew. Are you Open to that?"

"Yes."

"Think how many people can't leave their town and come to New York or Los Angeles to see our seminars. The closest they will ever get to Wholeness is speaking to you on the phone. But think how close *you* are." She rested her hand on his heart. "Do you want this?"

"Yes."

"Can you give us better than your best?"

"Yes, I can."

"Good," she said, giving his wrist two quick squeezes.

He opened his eyes.

"That's who I want here with me; the kind of man who becomes a Trainer. With your Power of Intention and your closing record, you could have what you came here to get. You could be a Leader." She got up and sat behind her desk. "Listen to the meditation on track two every day until you hear it in your head."

When Matthew walked out to the hallway, Deborah and Owen were getting onto the elevator.

Deborah's limp brown hair was pushed loosely off her forehead in a clip and she looked beat. She switched the plastic bag with the remnants of the snacks she had given Owen to eat during her shift to her other hand and yawned. Owen rubbed his eyes and as he did, he wobbled a little with the weight of the overstuffed backpack that hung from his shoulders.

"Whoa, that is one big bag." Matthew said. "What do you have in there?"

"I got the rocks and minerals I've been collecting, my comic books and also my circuit board." Owen seemed to strain to stand up straighter.

"A circuit board, that's what that was. I've never seen one like that before."

"You can help me with it if you want sometime."

"Sure, sounds fun."

Matthew held the door open for them as they stepped out of the lobby and onto the street. "Can I get you guys a cab?"

"We're taking the subway."

"In that case I'll walk you to your station."

"You don't have to, Matthew."

"Why do you always say that? Where I come from, guys make sure women and children get home safely."

"But you live in Queens. It's not even the right direction for you."

"It's fine. I need the air. Besides you two can't walk alone. It's late."

"Well, thanks, you're sweet. A real gentleman."

110

It was after midnight when Matthew dropped them off at their subway and began his walk back across town, but he wasn't tired. He was still buzzing inside like he'd just left a party. That's how he felt every time he finished work those weeks, jittery and a little drained but content with himself. There was no question this job was the best thing he had ever made happen.

His friends back home were all having babies too soon or messing around with women they were about to run out on. His cousins were living thousands of dollars in debt, working in restaurants or in construction looking forward to fifty-dollar employee bucks at Christmastime. That wasn't enough for him.

He had been raised not to ask for more than he had but as Genevieve taught, there was Enough for everyone. Everybody had the same Opportunity, it's what he or she did with it that mattered. And the part that he appreciated most was something that used to worry him: being successful didn't mean others had to suffer for it. It was his obligation to shine.

You couldn't just complain about your life, sit around hoping things would change. It's when you approached your life from a place of lack that trouble started; that's how you got stuck. If you wanted to transform your life you had to take responsibility for yourself. Yes, it took determination, but there was no end to what you could achieve. If people like Deborah could truly understand how amazing their Opportunity was, they would see success was for everyone.

Matthew listened to Genevieve's meditations, during his six-mile runs in the morning, on the subway, and again at night before bed. He could feel himself becoming healthier and stronger—he had even lost ten pounds. He didn't know anybody in the city outside the Team but that was all right, because with two shifts a day he didn't have time to do much else except exercise and travel to work and back.

Being among the mind-boggling array of people he passed in the street every day invigorated him. Back home, nobody was ever out past ten. Here somebody was always around, even at two in the morning they were on their way somewhere; men and women coming from work, from bars, from parties, all of them moving in every direction through the muggy night.

The damp air clung to him and the click of high heels drew nearer and farther again as Matthew made his way across town taking everything in. Grocers stood behind small check-out counters under the fluorescent lights of their corner markets, the overripe cantaloupe and sour cabbage smell of garbage sweating in shiny black bags came in waves as he passed it piled up high curb after curb, and the lit-up sky peered down on him from in between tall buildings; buildings in every height made of glass and of stone, unfolding as he approached, one after another, like possibility.

The city was not the tangled angry town his family

had warned him about, it was a jumble of opportunities beautiful in its way. Everything he wanted was in sight; it was only up to him how far he would go.

As soon as he got on the Seven train to Queens, he put on Genevieve's meditation and felt the liquid gold warmth of her voice moving through him, filling all the spaces inside.

 Track Two

"Do you remember the feeling of having it all? You might have to think back to another time, another place. When you were young and could still believe the world was for you. Before you had to explain yourself.

You could have anything then; all you had to do was choose.

Just by noticing, really noticing, a leaf. Or the clouds gliding swiftly across the crystal blue sky. The sound of the airplane humming above you. The smell of soil on your fingers. The buzzing of a lawn mower.

It all reminded you of how you were alive.

In those small moments you were complete and you experienced the expanding of yourself.

I want you to think about one of those

Home is a Made-Up Place complete moments now.

Do you have one?

Capture it.

Capture that feeling and hold it tight so you can crawl back and inhabit it.

Wear it like a new skin though it is older and truer than anything.

Look out of your face the same way you did then.

Use your hands the way you did back then.
I want you to *go into the world* the way you did then.
And see what happens.

See what happens when you stop investing in the unkindness you feed yourself, the unkindness you feel the world feeds you. The world *will* reflect what you believe.

What do you believe?"

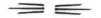

On Monday, the first day of the new sales cycle, the lobby door of the office opened after the shift had started and Ashley hurried in with her head down, adjusting the front of her dress. He didn't know how she managed in her shoes, her feet were almost vertical the heels were so high, but she wore them every day.

He waited until she had unloaded her big pleather bag off her shoulder and gotten settled. "Hey Ash, any idea what the record is for most packages sold in a month? I need to set my Intention."

She frowned.

"What? Why the look?"

"You're still doing that?"

"Of course, I am. Have been every day for two months. If you want to Live Better, you have to Do Better, right?"

"Easy does it, Elmira," she said picking up her headset, "that's a bit much this early."

The lobby door opened again and JC came in—he must have stepped out after distributing leads.

Matthew leaned in closer over their divider. "JC has the record, right?"

She searched his face as if she were checking for a trick. There were circles under her eyes and she had a half-inch of dark roots showing. Her hair was so bleached it had no substance, almost as if the only thing keeping it from blowing away was the piling up of it on top of itself.

"What's the number I have to beat?"

"Three hundred and eighty-six," she said and put her headset on.

"Three hundred and eighty-six? That's like twenty a shift."

"It can be done."

"Hey, you two chatting it up?" JC asked as he approached. "Don't let her distract you, Matty," he said putting his hand on the top of Ashley's head and squeezing it.

Ashley shot him a look and then dialed.

JC lifted his hand off her head and didn't move away until he saw that Matthew and Ashley had each gotten in touch with a lead.

Every day for the next four weeks Matthew set his Immediate, Future, and Ultimate Intentions: to beat his sales goal of the previous week, to become a Trainer by August, and, finally, to become a Leader; every night he fell asleep listening to Genevieve's meditations.

He was still amazed by The Plan, that all he had to do was believe and focus and he would see results. He was already coaching Deborah. He made a point of sharing some of his sales strategies with her on their walk to the subway after their shifts together. If she listened to what Genevieve was teaching and followed the techniques he gave her, she would absolutely be able to sell doubles. Once she started selling bigger packages, she would be able to clear the ten percent commission mark and there wouldn't be so much pressure on her.

It didn't seem fair that JC never gave Deborah a chance, that the people struggling the most to sell got the oldest, most used-up leads. It wasn't positive. Matthew bristled at how JC called her 2D, short for Dumpy Dog, or how he constantly undressed Ashley with his eyes—he was at least twice her age. Matthew couldn't fathom how someone as illuminated as Genevieve had ever tolerated JC. His slipperiness. Matthew knew he could be as good a Trainer as JC, better even. When he got promoted he would not shame his team, he'd take care of them.

Toward the end of July Deborah had started to listen to Matthew and was coming in early if her schedule permitted. She was already sitting in her seat when he arrived the last Monday of the sales cycle. He waved a hello and picked up his leads and when he got to his cubicle she leaned over her divider.

"Hey Matthew, I got two doubles and it's only been twenty minutes. Pretty good, huh?"

He high-fived her. "That's the way you do it."

There was a new picture from Owen on his corkboard and he waved to him across the room. Owen held up the rock Matthew had found for him at the edge of a construction site the week before. Matthew gave him the thumbs up and gestured he'd be over soon. He took a fresh lead sheet from his own stack of new ones, and passed it to Deborah. "Let me know when you're done with that one and I'll hook you up with another one."

Deborah's eyes lit up. "Really? Thanks."

Genevieve came over and put a cup of iced coffee in Matthew's hands. She pulled his chair out for him and rested her hand on his shoulder. "You need anything, Matthew?"

He put his headphones on. "Nope, I'm good."

"Are you ready to break yesterday's record?"

"Definitely."

She squeezed his shoulder and peered at Deborah from over the divider.

"Imagine if everybody here worked as hard." Deborah smiled up at her but Genevieve stared back until Deborah looked down at her notebook.

On July 31st, the last day of the sales cycle, Matthew picked up a slice of pizza across the street before coming in for the end of quarter bonus shift. He joined Ashley, who was standing outside the office building sipping from a canned protein drink and smoking.

He had never been in this neighborhood on a Saturday night; the street was more crowded than he'd seen it before. Pierced young men and women and heavily made-up groups of screeching girlfriends in tiny dresses passed by on their way to the clubs down the block.

A fire engine screamed by and right afterward a young woman stepped toward the curve and vomited in the gutter while a guy held her up. Someone across the street screamed that it was foul.

Ashley giggled.

"What?"

"I bet th—" Just then another flashing fire engine tore by, siren blaring. She waited until the group of club goers in front of them finished whooping and catcalling the firefighters who had waved back to them and continued. "I was about to say, I bet this kind of stuff makes you want to run back to Elmira."

"No way," he laughed. "All I've ever wanted to do is leave."

"Yeah?" She took a sip of her protein drink. "What did you even do up there—bag groceries at the general store or something?"

"Nice one." He wiped his mouth with a napkin. "No, I bartended, landscaped. Sold oil changes door to door, stuff like that."

"I think it's cute you're from the country. It makes you like, cleaner, somehow."

"Cleaner?" He shook his head. "Wow."

Ashley laughed again and nudged him with her shoulder. "Not cleaner, I mean more real. Like you're more trustworthy or something."

"I guess that's better."

"It is. You're not like the other guys around here," she said gesturing toward their office with a tilt of her head. She took a long drag of her cigarette. "I went upstate once," she said, exhaling away from him. "In sixth grade. My best friend's mom took us on a bus trip to Albany."

"What'd you think?"

"It was cold."

"That sounds right."

"The windows on the bus were fogged up like practically the whole time. Me and my friend had to keep wiping them with the sleeves of our shirts so we could see out even a little bit. I was psyched about going though, I remember really looking forward to leaving the city. To be getting away and going on a family trip—even though it wasn't actually my family. Which was good, my family sucks. I was like, *thank god*, I get to leave!"

"So it was fun?"

"I'm not sure. I think I spent most of the trip asking my friend's mom questions.

Like when would we be there, and how would we meet up with the group, and what would we see on the tour. I just kept asking her all these things. I could tell I was annoying her. And then even when we got to Albany and were touring the buildings and everything I still didn't stop. I asked her when we were going back to the bus and how long the ride would be and when we'd be home and all this stuff."

Ashley stubbed out her cigarette and Matthew dumped his paper plate in the garbage. They stepped onto the elevator together and she shook her head. "The whole thing was so dumb. I thought it would be so amazing to be away from home but as soon as we left I was all freaked out, I didn't know what to do with myself."

Matthew held the door to the office open.

"Just goes to show you."

"Show you what?"

"You can't escape who you are."

Matthew didn't think that was true and was about to say so when JC put his arm around her waist. "There she is. Walk with me."

Aside from Deborah, who was out taking care of Owen because he was sick with strep, the whole Team had come in for the bonus shift. The room was charged with energy and contact was good. Matthew got in touch with almost everyone he called and ended up selling doubles to all but two leads that purchased triples.

Near the end of the shift, Matthew glanced up when JC rolled a chair next to Ashley to listen in on her sales though she certainly didn't need help—she had been selling almost as well as Matthew lately. JC sat close up to her, lifted up one of her headphones, and began whispering in her ear. His face still close to Ashley's, his eyes shifted over to Matthew. "What you looking at, Matty? You know Ashley needs to be whipped into shape. Don't you, Ashley?"

Ashley's face burned red. Matthew's lead answered and he ducked his head toward his notebook to focus on his pitch.

JC had his head bent low to Ashley's notebook when Genevieve pulled a seat up next to Matthew. She waited for him to complete his call. "Well done, Matthew."

"Thanks." He took off his headphones.

She studied his face, her green eyes flickering. "Do you know what you did tonight?"

He had that feeling he got inside when he knew he was going to get what he wanted.

"You broke the record for most sales ever during a shift." She took both his hands in hers. "I'm going to invite you to be one of our Trainers."

His heart felt like it stopped. He was almost dizzy from the impact. This was what he had been working for; this was his second Intention coming true.

"Thank you, Genevieve," he said. He squeezed her hands. "I won't let you down."

"I know you won't."

From over the divider there was fumbling. Matthew heard Ashley gasp. Her head came back into view and she swatted in JC's direction "Stop," she hissed, "stop," and she stood up. Matthew was staring at the reddish-purple blotch on the side of her neck when she looked in his direction. She froze when she noticed Genevieve.

"Come, on," JC chided, "get back here." He moved to pull her back down and glanced in Matthew's direction. "Don't worry about Matty, he's—"

JC halted when he saw Genevieve. Within a moment he recovered and, switching gears, continued addressing Ashley. "—he's closing at his own pace. And that's exactly what you need to do. Like I keep telling you, Ashley."

Genevieve stood up. Her eyes moved over Ashley

and JC. Apart from what looked like a small twitch pulling her top lip, she was still. "Matthew," she said without taking her eyes off JC, "let's get you set up with training materials."

Ska was blasting in the office when Matthew got to work on Monday. Genevieve's office door was closed. Deborah's seat was empty. When Matthew got to his seat Ashley was in hers, holding a pile of old--looking lead sheets. She looked pale—even her make-up couldn't hide it. She was gnawing on one of the cuticles of her other hand.

"You okay?" he whispered.

"Yeah, yeah, I'm fine. Just tired."

He handed her a Recharge Vita-Pack from his desk.

"Thanks."

Genevieve's door opened and shut and JC came over without looking at Ashley. "How many you need, Matty?"

"It's Matthew."

Ashley lowered her head and started dialing.

"Fifteen." Matthew met his eyes. He couldn't tell if Genevieve had told JC she'd need Matthew to start training immediately.

"Let's go, then."

When JC walked away, Matthew handed Ashley a sheet of his choice leads.

Five minutes later Genevieve opened her door and entered the room wearing a peach silk blouse with the top two buttons open, her creamy string of pearls, and a close-fitting cream skirt. She must have had a Seminar that night.

"Oh good, Ashley's arrived. We can do our Meditation now. No, don't get up." She cut the music. "We'll do it here."

She went to the front of the room.

"I want you to look at yourself. Look at the way you are in the world. Do you move with direction and purpose? Or are you without aim? Worse," she said making her way past the cubicles, "are you barely moving? When others tell you their hopes, their dreams, do you hear them? Or does envy cinch you inside?

Those people are put in your way not to thwart you but to show you how much better you could be. Jealousy is a message. A message that there is something *you* are not doing." She continued surveying the room, but her eyes kept returning to Ashley. "Will you keep letting your life force trickle out of your diminished being, ruining it for everyone else? Or will you listen to the message your Higher Self is sending you?"

Genevieve stood at Matthew and Ashley's station. "Are you ready to admit you are not doing your best and offer yourself elsewhere until you're actually ready?" She focused on Ashley. "Can you do that so those around you can follow their own lit-up paths in peace? Don't make everybody watch as you wither and collapse and take what isn't yours. It's time you did something else."

Ashley stared back at Genevieve.

"Pack up your stuff, Ashley."

Ashley didn't move.

"Go on now."

Ashley cleared her throat. "What for?"

"For doubting The Plan. For creating bad energy. For not trying hard enough." Her eyes glimmered. "For being this version of yourself."

Genevieve perched on Ashley's desk. "I can continue unless you're ready to leave. You won't be coming back."

Ashley scanned the room looking, it seemed, for help.

Matthew's stomach dropped. From his seat he had already swept the room searching for JC but he was nowhere to be found. Except for the flutter of Ashley's eyes returning to confront Genevieve, she was frozen. It was quieter on the sales floor than it had ever been.

Ashley looked down at her desk and shook her head. Matthew saw her lips move as if she was saying something to herself. She took her headphones off and dropped them on her desk. She locked eyes with Matthew and stood up. She lifted her bag onto her shoulder and without another glance at the room full of people staring at her from over their dividers, without a toss of her head or flip of her hair, she walked out.

Work had ended but Matthew couldn't go home, not yet. He needed to get his head on straight. He'd tried to get in to talk to Genevieve about Ashley but she had left for a three-day Seminar sometime during the shift.

He crossed west and when he hit the meatpacking district, he walked along the river. Lights twinkled endlessly in tiny dots over the Hudson, apartments with their windows stacked on top of themselves row after row. Everything looked the same tonight, but it wasn't.

He could have easily caught the Seven train but kept walking through the glass and steel of midtown. Then toward the old high rises and brownstones of the Upper West Side, the buildings crafted as ornately as wedding cakes; flowers carved into their faces, silent twirling vines jutting from their eves.

North now he headed to Central Park, the dark canopy of trees knitted together and rustling above him, stirring the overripe honeyed smell of the summer night as they lunged over their stone walls in the dark. He stumbled on an uneven crack in the sidewalk and felt a piece of pavement move under him with a low clunk. A small corner of the cement had separated from the rest of its squared off section. Matthew picked it up. He never got enough of how the flecks of mica in the pavement up here glittered with so little available light. He dropped the corner into his bag for Owen.

When Matthew got back to his sublet he boiled up

half a box of spaghetti and dumped half a jar of sauce on it. The air conditioner was still broken so he went down to the front stoop with his dinner. Genevieve had given the Team refocus homework after the negativity of the day. They were each to pay careful attention to Meditation 4 before returning to work tomorrow, especially because she was traveling and couldn't be there to lead them personally. Matthew knew he needed to stop thinking about the chaos of the day, the tug he felt inside. He had no way of contacting Ashley; he didn't even know her last name. He put on his headphones and listened to the meditation as he ate his dinner, trying to ignore the giant roaches that scurried by.

 Track Four

People are responsible for themselves.

Do good work and help support those struggling around you but, do not entrap yourself in pity.

It will immobilize you.

You don't have to listen to the news or feel responsible for bad things that happen to people. *You* are your only responsibility. If you do your work, just yours, you will create your own good life. And what a contribution that will be to the world. That is real living. If people get insecure or unhappy because you

are succeeding, that is their own Deficiency. That is
chatter and noise.
It is victimhood. It is fear.

Are you afraid of yourself?

Of what you could become?

What would happen if you actually
created what you want?

Who would you be then?

Those that are afraid of themselves will balk, they'll
complain. Because when you do what *you* need to do
you are bound to make others interrogate themselves.

Do most people want to do that? Not really.

You will know you're doing well because others will
doubt you, they'll shake their heads
about how you're changing.

And they will either push back or they will fall away.

But don't you stop.
What the planet needs are more people who take
responsibility for their happiness, Satisfied people who
own their power.

This is the key: When you take care of yourself, you *are* taking care of the world and that *is* taking care of others.

Claim your power. Claim what is yours.

On Thursday of that same week Matthew came in and walked past the percolating coffee, past the frosted donuts in their hot pink box, past a new girl in reception and right over to Deborah to welcome her back. It had been a week since he'd seen her. Now that Owen was starting to feel better, she'd left him with a neighbor so she could make her shift. When Matthew dropped his stuff on his desk he saw a note from Genevieve to come see her. And then he noticed all the pictures Owen had made for him had been taken down.

Genevieve opened the door as soon as Matthew knocked. "Great," she smiled, "you're here. Ready to start training?"

"Definitely. Hey Genevieve, do you know why all the pictures are off my board?"

"The ones what's-his-name drew?"

"Owen."

"That's right, Owen. We're going to be doing a little energy housekeeping. You know, cleaning up the Team. We didn't want that type of emotional clutter to get in your way.

"Cleaning up the Team. But what does Owen have to do with—wait. You don't mean Deborah?"

"I wasn't going to bog you down with that, but yes."

"But she's getting her numbers up, I've been helping her."

She reached for his hand. "Oh, sweet Matthew."

"No really, did you see the doubles she's gotten this month?"

"I'm afraid with the missed shifts and the negative energy she's saddled us with, it's just not enough."

"But, how can you say that? She's been working hard."

She stared at him without registering his words.

He tried again. "She's been here for two years. What is she going to do without this job, Genevieve?"

"Not my problem."

A tall, muscular young man Matthew had never seen before rapped on the open door.

"Oh good," she smiled, "Tanner's here. Matthew, this is Tanner. You'll be training him today. Please take him to reception for his headphones."

"Genevieve, I'd really like to talk about this."

"Sure, doll, come on back after the shift," she said shutting her door.

Matthew was at Ashley's old desk training Tanner in a fog, knowing they were about to fire Deborah. He had already knocked on Genevieve's door again and was about to go back when the new girl in reception came over to his desk. Her headset was still on, the wire dangling in front of her pilling acrylic cardigan.

"Matthew, right? You've got a phone call. She says she's been trying to reach you."

Ashley. He went to his own desk to snap his headset in and fumbled the buttons.

"This is Matthew."

There was a pause.

"Ashley?" he whispered.

"No, this is Brenda."

"Brenda." He said.

"In Baton Rouge. You sold me my pills."

"Yes, Brenda! Brenda, how are you?"

"I've been trying to reach you for days. But they told me you were unavailable."

"Oh, I'm sorry, I didn't get any messages."

"Every time that's what they said: 'he's unavailable.'"

"I'm really sorry about that."

Tanner was listening in with his own headset.

"Well, I'm glad I'm here now to take your call and get your reorder in. Let's set you up with a double, I'm sure you're running low on pills by now."

"I stopped taking them."

He pointed to page three in his script to show Tanner where he was. "Well, they're not going to work if you don't take them, Brenda."

"The doctor thinks that's why I lost my baby."

"Excuse me?"

He heard her intake of breath over the line. JC dashed by with a pile of order sheets flapping behind him. He pointed his index finger at Matthew mid-stride. "Got one?"

Matthew stared at him.

"My baby."

"Did you say—"

"My doctor thinks it was them capsules. The Pennyroyal and the Peruvian bark in the capsules that hurt her."

"I, I, when did this happen?" He heard himself asking, as if it made a difference.

"Brenda?" Matthew heard her sobbing. "I'm—I'm so sorry."

JC came over. "What's going on? Who are you talking to?"

"I had a feeling I shouldn't take them." She said through sobs. "But I believed you. I didn't listen to my own self."

Genevieve came out of her office and grabbed Tanner's training headset to listen in.

"I'm so sorry, Brenda," Matthew said.

JC was closer now. "What are you doing, get off the line."

"Hang up the line, Matt," Genevieve warned.

"I shouldn't have trusted you."

Genevieve pulled out Matt's line and switched over the channels. "Ma'am, this is the Resources department. You'll refer to our labels which suggest you check with a doctor before starting this or any program."

"But you all said I could take them even if I was

pregnant."

"I am sure that is not what we said. We are very sorry for your loss. When you're ready to take responsibility for yourself, when you are ready to make The Plan work, we will be here. Take care of yourself." And she hung up.

Matthew rose to his feet. "What are you doing? I wasn't done talking to her."

"Yes. You were."

"No, I wasn't. You can't do that!"

"Really." She crossed her arms. "What does that look like, Matthew?"

"I'm her rep, Genevieve."

"This is my program." She handed Matthew's leads to JC. "I think you should go to the Studio and take a break."

"No."

"Matthew. You're going to leave the floor now and go to the Focus Studio."

"I don't think so, Genevieve."

The others on the Team had been hunched over their laminated sales sheets, flipping pages with their headsets cradling their heads, pretending not to notice what was happening, but now, for the second time that week, they gaped wide-eyed at the spectacle.

JC reached for Matthew's left arm. "Come with me."

Matthew shrugged him off.

JC grabbed his arm. "Let's go, buddy."

"Stay away from me, JC," Matthew said, pushing

him off hard enough that JC lost his balance. He tipped backwards and as he tried to steady himself, he bumped into Genevieve. She shoved him off to protect herself and his foot caught on the leg of a chair. His arms waving in the air, he tried to recover his balance, but was too late and landed on the floor.

The room was silent.

Genevieve's face was flushed. Her nostrils flaring, she adjusted her posture and smoothed out her top.

JC got back up a few seconds after he landed and made a lunge for Matthew. Genevieve waved him back with her arm and kept it there until JC stopped where he was.

"What a shame," she announced in a louder voice than usual. She climbed onto a desk so she could see the Team better. "A real waste. It seems Matthew has forgotten everything we taught him."

"Please, Genevieve," he said.

"What you're doing right now, Matthew, is not The Plan. Tanner, Everybody," she scanned the room, "Matthew is so close to success and what's happening? He's letting his Doubt take over. He isn't listening for Answ—"

"Just stop, Genevieve," Matthew said interrupting her.

He met her blazing eyes, and for the first time in the months he'd known her, they didn't unhinge him. "You don't have any answers. You just hurt people."

He picked up his bag and went to Deborah who had been watching everything with worried eyes. "You should go too," he whispered to her.

From his bag he pulled out the chipped-off piece of sidewalk he'd been saving for Owen. "Would you give this to him for me?" He placed it in her hand, the flecks of mica flickering throughout its surface, the boundlessness he hoped Owen would recognize even in that locked up space.

As soon as Matthew stepped outside the hot morning wrapped itself around him. Horns blared in the clogged-up street, delivery trucks moved and stopped again with the high pitched, splintering sound of their worn-out breaks, taxis crawled across town, jaywalkers darting between them.

He joined the rush of people bustling around him, their faces suspended in thought, their worries and hopes, anger and sadness, their dreams swirling around together as their bodies carried them forward. All of them finding their own way, even when that could be the hardest thing to do.

Acknowledgements

"House in the Woods" first appeared in *American Literary Review* and was runner up for the 2015 American Literary Review Award for Fiction and a finalist in Third Coast Magazine's 2015 Jaimy Gordon Prize for Fiction.

"Gibbous" first appeared in *Best New Writing 2014* and won the Eric Hoffer Award for Prose and was a finalist in *Narrative's* Winter 2014 Short Story Contest.

"Rick's Wax Hands" first appeared in *The Iowa Review* and was runner up for The Iowa Review Award for Fiction selected by ZZ Packer.

"What February Feels Like" first appeared in *Red Fez* and was nominated for a Pushcart Prize.

"The Plan" first appeared in Sequestrum and was winner of the 2016 Sequestrum Award for New Writers.

Thank you to the fiction teachers I've had the privilege of studying with: Scott Driscoll at the University of Washington's certificate program where I wrote my first story, Marie-Helene Bertino at One Story's Summer Conference, Anna Balint and Cara Diaconoff at Hugo House, Pete Fromm and Jack Driscoll at Pacific University's MFA program and to Cate Kennedy who I didn't have the chance to study with but from whom I learned so much. And extra special thanks again to both Cate Kennedy and Marie-Helene Bertino for reading this collection.

Thank you to the many workshop groups and readers who put up with my early drafts when I was first cutting my teeth. There's a reason I attached candy to some of those stories and I am grateful for your generosity. Special thanks to Jennifer Fliss.

Thank you to my publisher Diane Windsor at Motina Books Publishing who is a pleasure to collaborate with and has championed my work from the start.

Thank you to my virtual writing community for your friendship, encouragement, support, and fun messages at all hours from the Podstars. Special thanks to Allison K. Williams and Ashleigh Renard for connecting so many of us. To Danielle Simone Brand, Virginia Alice Crawford, Melissa Gould, Ari Honarvar, Estelle Erasmus, Jo-Ann Finkelstein, Elizabeth Heise, Diana Kupershmit, Debi Lewis, Amy Long of Taylor Swift as Books, Jamie McGillen, Lindsay Merbaum, Alyson Shelton, Traci Skuce, Kara Tatelbaum, Dana Van Nest, my memoir sister Keema Waterfield, Stephanie Weaver, and Michelle Yang, thank you for your encouragement, generosity, and kindness.

To my dear friends who have seen me change careers, cities, and genres and encouraged me all these years: so much of what I've learned because of you has made its way to these pages. Thank you, Elissa, Eliza, Heather, Rachel, Sondy, Star, The Binghamton Maries: Alison, Lauren, Marie and Joe, Dawn, Cynthia, Kim, Ali and Kris, Carrie, Lily, Tali, Winter, Alice, Birgit, Leslie, Meg, Missy, Rachel, and Jen S. for sticking with me as I found more of myself.

Thank you to my sister, my parents, my aunts, cousins, uncles, and grandparents for helping me discover and listen to the voices that have informed my creative life.

Thank you to my daughter and my son for being who you are. Words can't really capture how much I love you. I adore you! You make my life full and happy and sometimes you even laugh at my jokes. Really appreciate that, kids.

Thank you to my husband who is the best husband. Every day I'm grateful for you and love you more.

About the Author

Photo: Sarah Anne Photography

Ronit Plank is a Seattle-based writer, teacher, and editor whose work has been featured in *The Atlantic, The Washington Post, The New York Times, Writer's Digest, The Rumpus, American Literary Review, Hippocampus, The Iowa Review,* and elsewhere. Her stories and essays have been nominated for the Pushcart Prize, the Best of the Net, and the Best Microfiction Anthology. Her first book is *When She Comes Back,* a memoir about the loss of her mother to the guru Bhagwan Shree Rajneesh and their eventual reconciliation. Her weekly podcast, *Let's Talk Memoir,* features interviews with memoirists about craft, the creative process, and the writing life and is available on Apple, Spotify, and at ronitplank.com.

CPSIA information can be obtained
at www.ICGtesting.com
Printed in the USA
BVHW032317130223
658422BV00004B/89